Elderberry thicket /

3 5086 00114 3500

P9-DGG-113

Z343e

The Elderberry Thicket

The Elderberry Thicket

JOAN T. ZEIER

Atheneum   1990   New York

Collier Macmillan Canada

TORONTO

Maxwell Macmillan International Publishing Group

NEW YORK   OXFORD   SINGAPORE   SYDNEY

To my family

Copyright © 1990 by Joan T. Zeier

All rights reserved. No part of this book may be reproduced or
transmitted in any form or by any means, electronic or mechanical,
including photocopying, recording, or by any information storage and
retrieval system, without permission in writing from the publisher.

Atheneum
Macmillan Publishing Company
866 Third Avenue
New York, New York 10022

Collier Macmillan Canada, Inc.
1200 Eglinton Avenue East
Suite 200
Don Mills, Ontario M3C 3N1

First Edition
Printed in the United States of America
Designed by Trish Parcell Watts
10 9 8 7 6 5 4 3 2 1

Library of Congress Cataloging-in-Publication Data
Zeier, Joan T.
The elderberry thicket / Joan T. Zeier. —1st ed. p. cm.
Summary: In 1938 Wisconsin, when twelve-year-old Franny's father
loses his job as a hired hand and has to go looking for work, the
family members doubt their self-reliance as they face again the hard
times they had hoped were gone for good.
ISBN 0–689–31612–7
[1. Self-reliance—Fiction. 2. Country life—Fiction.
3. Wisconsin—Fiction.] I. Title. PZ7.Z3935E1 1990
[Fic]—dc20 90–90 CIP AC

Contents

CHAPTER 1

To Call Our Own

Franny saw her mother's head jerk up even before she heard the door open or felt the rush of winter air.

"Did you find out anything, James?" asked Mama. "What's wrong?" Her voice was shrill, scared sounding.

Papa stepped into the kitchen. He pulled off his wool cap with the flannel-lined earflaps and grinned at twelve-year-old Franny.

"Is your mama worrying about nothin' again? You ladies can just keep on peeling your potatoes and ease your minds. Mr. Copper had to go off on some family matter—that's all."

"But he's never gone off like that before." Mama's knife jabbed at the potato in her hand. "He shouldn't have left you to milk all his cows by yourself."

"Now, Rosalyn, I can handle the milking. That's what a hired man is *for*. Carl Copper got a long-distance call from his sister in Milwaukee and had to leave. Maybe she's sick or something. They really didn't say."

"It just seems like something's wrong," Mama fretted. "Why is it such a secret? Did Mrs. Copper go, too?"

Papa chuckled. "He wouldn't go without *her.*"

He had great respect for Mrs. Copper, but sometimes he and Mama made little jokes about the way she bossed her husband. Papa seemed to have a reasonable answer about their trip. Franny knew her mother was a worrier. Still, it bothered her some.

"Say, Franny," Papa said, changing the subject. "Since I've got all those chores to do, I could use a helper. Want to come over to the farm with me?"

"You bet!" Franny threw down her potato and jumped up, but he held up his arm.

"Whooo-oa now, Franny. Hold your horses. The cows will wait until you finish your work."

Franny shook her long brown pigtails impatiently. Luckily, there were only two potatoes left.

"Can I come, too?" asked four-year-old Martin, who was playing on the wooden floor with Baby Sarah. He didn't look as though he wanted to stop playing, but he always asked, anyway.

"Not this time, Martin," said Papa. "Maybe tomorrow, if Mr. Copper hasn't come back."

Franny gave the last potato a few quick slashes and plunked it in the kettle.

"Don't get your coat dirty in the barn," Mama warned.

She did not need to say it. Franny was proud of her blue wool coat. It was the warmest one she'd ever had and it didn't bother her at all that someone else had outgrown it and given it to the used clothing shop. The snow pants were another story. Mrs. Copper had made them from some of Mr. Copper's old trousers. Franny had to admit they were warm, but she could hardly wait for spring so she could hide them in a closet. She stuffed them into her patched-up boots, grabbed her cap and mittens, and followed Papa outside.

Mr. Copper's tidy farmyard was only a quarter-mile down the road, but they drove the old rattletrap truck they'd bought just before they left Chicago. With a sly grin, Papa whipped the steering wheel toward the driveway without braking, but Franny held tight to the seat and didn't even squeal. Papa should know by now that she was no scaredy-cat.

The cows stood near the barn in a woeful half-circle, tails to the cold wind, waiting while fresh straw was spread and their mangers filled with hay. Then Franny had to climb out of the way up on the hay chute, while Papa opened the door for the impatient herd. When they had all jostled their way into the stanchions, she climbed down and made a bed for herself in a little pile of hay, where the *pring, pring, pring* of milk hitting the bucket almost put her to sleep.

She loved the warm, sweet smell of hay and the gentle cow sounds. Munching and bumping together, the herd reminded her of a human family. Content, comfortable, secure.

When Papa had finished milking and put the cans down in the milk house, they got back into the truck. He was whistling a little tune, and after he'd started the motor, he had such a pleased look on his face that Franny wasn't even surprised when he asked, "Whaddya say we go to town and get some ice cream?"

She didn't hesitate. "Let's go!" she said. "I guess we must be in the money, huh?"

Papa smiled. "I just think we need a little celebration. It's been a year now since we came to Fisher's Glen."

"A year? Seems like we've always lived here."

"Come on, Franny. You must remember Chicago!"

"I don't *want* to remember Chicago." She wrinkled up her nose. "Bugs in our hotel room and eating out of grocery bags."

"A little hardship is good for people—it builds character." Papa grinned and the flash of white teeth made him look young. "But I'll admit, ten years' worth of character was enough for me."

"Remember the look on Mama's face when she first saw our house?" Franny asked. "I thought for a minute she was going to choke."

"Your mama still hasn't gotten over her fancy bringing up," Papa said, shaking his head. "She saw an old, dirty, abandoned farmhouse with a holey roof. *I* saw a mansion that just needed some spare parts."

Franny giggled. "Not quite a mansion, Papa."

"Well, I ain't *done* with it yet." He looked a little hurt. "I promised your mama a long time ago that I'd take good care of her. Things never worked out like I planned, with the Depression and all, but a few more trips to the dump and we'll be living in high style. I'll bet Mrs. Webster will throw away a lot of good stuff again this spring."

"I'll bet so, too," agreed Franny. Alice Faye Webster was her best friend and she'd been in their house lots of times. Alice Faye had a ruffled bedspread with matching curtains, just like in the catalog, and everything in their house was new and pretty. Of course, Mr. Webster owned the lumberyard and always had money.

Papa's "mansion" was only a few hundred feet through a patch of scrub oak and elderberry bushes from the end of Elm Street, where the Websters lived. Franny could run over there in ten minutes. But to get to town by car, you had to take the road that circled around Heddler's Bluff—a good two miles.

They got the ice cream at Benson's Drugstore, and Franny was proud to march in there with her papa, even if he was wearing his faded denim chore clothes. Lots of people were in town on Saturday night and she could just imagine them whispering, "Who's that girl in the blue coat? She surely has a handsome father. And buying ice cream, too. They must be having a party."

It was suppertime when they got home, so they hid the ice cream in a half-melted pile of snow until they had finished eating. Franny watched Martin's eyes light up when Papa brought in the surprise. Mama gasped, and even Baby Sarah was delighted.

"Special occasion," explained Papa. "Exactly one year ago Mr. Copper found the best hired man in the state of Wisconsin."

"And that's how you got to be a farmer," said Martin, repeating part of the story Papa liked to tell.

"That's right," Papa agreed. "I got to be a farmer *and* a builder *and* a gardener—and as soon as we finish this ice cream, I'm going to be a musician!"

Franny and Martin clapped their hands. They loved music, especially when Papa got out his guitar and sang with them.

The Coppers had given them a battery radio from their attic, so they'd learned a lot of new songs from the "WLS Barndance" and "Grand Ole Opry," as well as the old favorites from the school songbook.

They gathered around Papa in the middle of the kitchen while he fussed with the strings until the sound suited him. Then he looked up. "What's first?"

" 'I Want to Be a Cowboy's Sweetheart,' " Franny said.

"All right—now, don't forget to *project*." Papa started strumming and they all sang as loud as they could.

Except Mama, of course. She always said she had no

singing voice at all, so she sat quietly rocking, nursing the baby and smiling a little.

Martin didn't know all the words, but he didn't let that stop him—when you're four, you learn fast. As soon as they finished, he asked for "Noah's Ark."

Then it was "Darling Clementine" (all the verses), "I've Been Workin' on the Railroad," "Bye, Bye, Blackbird," which was Papa's favorite, and one after another until they couldn't think of any more songs and their voices began to strain.

"Now let's let Mama pick the last one," said Papa, leaning forward, the lamplight reflecting in his blue eyes. "What'll it be, Rosalyn?"

"Oh, I don't know—" Mama seemed embarrassed. "It all sounds so nice—maybe 'Let the Rest of the World Go By.' Can you play that, James?"

"I'll sure try," Papa said, and began searching for the right chords.

"I don't know that one," complained Franny.

"Then you'll have to learn it," said Papa gently, and began to sing the song Mama had asked for—slowly and softly—just for her.

The old cast-iron cookstove that came with the house was still keeping the kitchen cozy, and little tongues of flame shone through the chrome window to one side of the grate. Franny wished she had a camera to take a picture, but she knew she'd never forget it, anyway. Papa, in his thick plaid shirt, was squatting on a round block of wood near the stove, cradling his guitar, while

Martin, on a smaller block, was resting his curly head against Papa's knee. Mama, her pale face really beautiful in the dim light, was holding Sarah, asleep on her shoulder, a blanket pulled around the two of them. Even Mama had stopped worrying. It must have been nothing, after all, this trip of the Coppers'.

And Franny. Lucky Franny Parsons, the happiest twelve-year-old in the world. Nothing could ever spoil what she felt.

"A place that's known to God alone—just a spot to call our own," Papa's low voice continued.

"Oh, Papa," Franny wanted to say. "You found it for us, right here in Fisher's Glen. Our own house, the nice people from church who gave us things to make it homey—Julia Jarvis, who helped Mama when there was no doctor to deliver Sarah—and the school with singing every morning—thank you, God, for showing Papa this home for us."

"And let the rest of the world go by . . ." When he finished singing, Papa must have been thinking some of the same things, because his face had a very tender look about it and he asked gruffly, "Shall we say a prayer together?"

They all nodded and bowed their heads while he did the talking.

"Thank you, God. You've more than answered all my prayers—all the things I asked for just over a year ago. Please keep on watchin' over us—make us worthy of all the good things You've done for us—and don't let any of us forget it was You who done it. Amen."

Franny didn't move. She wouldn't have wanted to be the one to break the magic, but Papa rose slowly and touched Martin's shoulder lovingly. Then he went to Mama, took Sarah from her, and headed toward the alcove where her homemade crib stood. It was bedtime, but before she went, Franny got out a red crayon and put a heart on the calendar—Saturday, March 5, 1938—so she wouldn't forget what a good time they had had.

On Sunday, the Coppers still weren't back, so Papa got Martin and Franny up early and took them to the farm. Mr. Copper was always afraid the children would get hurt, but Papa knew they could be trusted and liked having them with him while he did the chores. It seemed like their very own farm, where they could do what they liked.

Mrs. Copper kept a small flock of chickens—just enough to supply both families with eggs. They were nervous from being cooped up all winter and made a terrible racket when Franny and Martin opened the door and slipped in with a pail of chicken feed. They filled the feeders and, while the noisy hens fought for their share, checked the nests and carefully placed the dozen or so warm eggs into the egg bucket.

Meanwhile, Papa had let the horses into the barnyard while he cleaned their stalls. They were huge, sturdy animals—the gray dappled work team, and black Jupiter, only slightly smaller, who was used singly or as a third hitch for heavy work. They enjoyed the freedom of being outside, even in cold weather, where they could spend the day kicking, taking short gallops around the barnyard, and flexing their powerful muscles.

Stretching their necks across the heavy wooden fence for the ears of corn that Papa offered them, they seemed quite docile and the children were even brave enough to pat their velvet noses. Still, Franny knew they could be dangerous, because of their size. And she had seen Jupiter roll his eyes in a way that told her, even better than Papa could, to be wary.

"Can we play with Jack now?" asked Martin, who was already tired of farm work.

Jack, the Coppers' dog, was twisting his body into a whirlwind of black, tan, and white at the end of his leash, the shaggy tail waving wildly. Every few minutes, he let out a yip to further remind everyone that he wanted some attention.

"All right, you can get him some of the scraps that Mrs. Copper saves for him in the summer kitchen. Unsnap his chain and let him run for a bit, too. The old mongrel's gettin' tired of being tied up. I've got to go and tend to the sheep yet."

Jack nearly knocked them down in his joy at being freed and ran in wild circles while Franny and Martin fixed a pan of table scraps for him. He wolfed down the food and then romped with them until Papa had finished all the morning chores.

Jack's eyes pleaded not to be tied up again, but Papa

reminded the children that they had to hurry home and get ready for church, so they gave the dog a last hug, snapped his chain, and started walking home. They were almost there when Papa pointed to a car approaching in the distance.

"Looks like the Coppers coming home," he said. "Funny they didn't stay until tonight."

When the car got closer, they saw that Papa was right (not that they had really doubted him), and waved a hearty welcome. Martin hopped up and down so they'd be sure to see him.

The car passed by as though the passengers had not seen them. In the front seat next to Mr. Copper was a strange young man, and Mrs. Copper was weighting down the backseat. None of them smiled, but looked straight ahead as they drove on toward their farm.

Papa looked puzzled. "They didn't look right to me," he said. "Something must have happened in Milwaukee. I sure hope their family's not in trouble."

"They drove right past us without waving," said Franny. "They *always* wave to us. And I wonder who that man is. I've never seen him before."

"Well, I'll find out tonight when I go to do chores," Papa replied. But there was a frown on his face as they hurried on, hopping over the early spring ruts that had formed in the driveway, anxious as always to reach the patched-up, weather-beaten house they had grown to love so much. Their home.

CHAPTER 2

Broken Promises

At suppertime, Papa hadn't come home from doing chores yet, so Mama dished up the soup and they ate without him. Supper wasn't any fun without Papa. Mama wasn't much for making conversation, and without Papa to egg them on, Martin and Franny were quieter than usual. They finished eating in no time.

"Did you have any homework this weekend?" Mama asked, when the dishes had been cleared away.

"Oh, darn!" Franny wrinkled up her nose in disgust. "I forgot *again.*" She had been looking forward to curling up by the stove with a library book, but realized there were two whole pages of arithmetic problems to do first.

"I don't see why Miss Snyder gives us such long assignments. I always get them right, anyway. She just likes to make us work," she grumbled, arranging her book and paper on a corner of the oilcloth-covered table.

It was nearly seven-thirty when she finished, and she was totally engrossed in her library book by the time Papa came in. He looked tired and didn't talk while he ate his supper, but the story Franny was reading was so exciting she wouldn't have noticed, anyway. It was about a wolf named Lobo whose life constantly depended upon his ability to outwit the humans who hunted him.

Mama finally had to take the book out of Franny's hands to make her go to bed. Franny's sympathies were entirely with Lobo, and she drifted off to sleep with fantasies of intelligent yellow eyes and the muffled yipping of the pack surrounding her.

Sometime later she woke suddenly, startled and confused, imagining again the whimper of the wolves. By the time she opened her eyes, she knew it was not a dream. The sound she heard was her mama crying. Her first thought was that her mother was sick, or hurting, like when Baby Sarah was born. But this was a different kind of sound—more like whimpers of despair—a moment of silence, like she was trying to hold it back, and another burst of sobs when she couldn't. Then there was Papa's kind voice—soothing—saying something so quietly Franny couldn't make it out—then the sobs again.

Franny lay still, straining her ears, afraid of what she was hearing. She thought of going out to the kitchen where the sounds were coming from, but didn't dare.

Mama's sobs continued and Franny started to shiver. Pulling the ragged blanket over her ears, she moved closer to Martin's warm, solid body. It would take a lot more than soft voices to wake a sound sleeper like Martin.

With her eyes wide open, all Franny could see was a dim line of light under the door. Papa had covered the window with layers of rags and cardboard to keep out the wind. Sometimes the ice-tipped fingers of the apple tree tapped against the glass, but from November until April, the children never saw moonlight at all.

For a long time Franny listened, hoping for some comforting explanation. She knew Papa was an orphan, but there could be bad news from Mama's family. There *were* grandparents somewhere, even though the only time anybody mentioned them was when she, Franny, lost her temper. Then it was usually Papa who would chide her gently: "You're acting just like your grandmother, Franny." Now Franny decided her grandfather must have died. Or maybe the spitfire grandmother. They would explain it all in the morning. After a little while, the light under the door disappeared and she heard them going to bed. Snuggling up to Martin, Franny closed her eyes.

When she awoke the next morning, everything seemed normal. The bedroom door was open—Papa always opened it in the morning so they could see to get up—and he was banging the grates, starting a fire in the old cookstove.

"All fired up for breakfast," he called out cheerfully a little while later. That was the signal every day to crawl out of bed and get dressed. Martin's eyes were still tightly closed, so Franny poked him, stepped out onto the chilly floor, grabbed her clothes off the chair, and headed for the warmth of the crackling cookstove.

Mama was stirring a kettle of oatmeal. Papa squatted on his block of wood next to the stove and reached out to give Franny a hug, just like always. It was like every other morning, and she had almost decided it had been a bad dream after all, until Mama turned to put the dishes on the table. Her mama's eyes were red and puffy.

Franny started feeling scared again. Slowly pulling her stockings on over the long underwear she had worn to bed, she waited. Surely they would tell her.

"Where's Martin?" asked Papa. "Don't tell me the bedbugs ate him!" Even his jokes were the same.

That brought a giggle from the children's bedroom. Martin, his smile accenting his dimples, shuffled out, dragging his clothes behind him. Even at a time like this, Franny could not help envying Martin's good looks. His round, trusting little face made everyone love him.

Papa moved the smaller block of wood for him to sit on and helped sort out his clothes. Martin was proud of being able to dress himself, but sometimes he got things inside out—or even upside down—if someone didn't help a little.

Franny buttoned her blue-checked dress and pulled on the red sweater—her best Christmas gift. It was already getting frayed around the sleeves from being worn so often. She stared at Mama, trying to catch her eye. But Mama was busy and was not looking at anyone.

She would just have to blurt it out. "Have you heard from Grandma and Grandpa lately?"

The question caught Mama by surprise, and a glob of oatmeal fell from the wooden spoon, back into the kettle.

"N-no. They don't—have time to write. Why do you ask?" The red-rimmed eyes showed alarm.

"No reason. I was just thinking about them." Franny tied her shoe carefully, avoiding the knots in the shoestring, which had already broken twice.

From the corner of her eye she saw them exchange glances. Papa coughed. Franny raised her head and looked to him for reassurance.

He sat hunched on the block of wood, his wide shoulders as solid as ever; and his sandy red hair curled around the edges of his face like it always did when it needed cutting. But something was different. There were lines on his forehead that Franny was not used to seeing, and worry in the soft blue eyes. She thought he was going to say something, but he changed his mind and turned his attention to Martin.

Whatever it is, why don't they tell me? thought Franny. *No matter how awful it is, I'd rather have them tell me than go off to school without knowing.*

They all sat down around the table, but Franny knew

without trying that the oatmeal was going to stick in her throat. Martin spooned his into his mouth as fast as he could, but Mama and Papa seemed to be having trouble, too, and poked at it quietly.

Franny couldn't wait any longer. She dropped her spoon against the edge of her bowl, and her voice came out brittle and shaky.

"I know something has happened. Please tell me what it is."

They all looked at her. Even Martin stopped eating. Papa's face was perplexed as he searched for words, and Mama covered her face with her hands.

"Well, Franny—" Papa began uncertainly and then tried to force the old cheerfulness into his voice. "Now, I don't want you to worry. We just have a little change in plans, but it's going to work out. I wasn't going to say anything until I could tell you something definite. . . ."

"Do we have to move?" Might as well ask the hardest question first—get it out in the open.

He was shaking his head. "No, no—no, Franny. See, Mr. Copper isn't gonna need me this year after all so I'm going to have to find something else. But he said we can just go on living here as long as we want. It's kind of sudden, and I'll have to look around a bit, but I'm sure to find some kind of work and then I can pay him rent."

"But Mr. Copper said you were the best hired man he ever had! Why won't he need you?"

"It's not his fault. He didn't want to let me go, but his

sister asked him a favor and he couldn't say no to her. His nephew needs work bad, and he can't hire *two* men."

"But *you* need work, too! And it was *your* job."

"Blood is thicker than water, Franny. And there's more to it than that. We should thank him for letting us live here."

"Oh, Papa!" So many feelings were battling inside her. How could they do something like this to Papa—to all of them? And didn't her parents even intend to put up a fight?

Mama had started sniffling into her handkerchief, but that was not what Franny felt like doing. She pushed away from the table and stomped across the floor. Mad! That was how she felt—mad!

CHAPTER 3

A Step at a Time

It was a little early to start for school, but Franny had to get out of the house. Mama's sniffling made her want to *do* something—something wild like running down to Coppers' and throwing a rock through their window—something she'd surely be sorry for later. Angrily she stuffed her books into her bag and thrust one leg at a time into the ugly snow pants, hoping to tear out Mrs. Copper's sturdy stitching, but the thread seemed to be made of steel. Flinging on her coat and scarf, she started for the door.

"Franny." Papa's voice was kind, but firm. "Come over here a minute."

She walked slowly toward him, not meeting his eyes. He took her hand and squeezed it through the mitten.

"Honey, don't leave with your chin stuck out like that—mercy sakes, it reminds me of your grandmother! But I love you, so please have faith—believe me, honey, it's going to be all right. As long as we stick together, things will work out."

Standing there with her hand in his, listening to his familiar voice, Franny believed him. Throwing her arms around Papa's neck, she pressed her face against his scratchy cheek. He hugged her close for a minute and coaxed a parting smile from her.

But by the time she had reached the path through the elderberry thicket, the surge of confidence had worn off.

"Who is he trying to fool?" she whispered. "There are no jobs around here. All everybody talks about is hard times."

And the smaller the town, the fewer jobs there were. In a little place like Fisher's Glen, anyone who had a job held on to it for dear life.

It was quiet in the thicket, and out of habit she stopped. The network of rodent paths was wearing through the vanishing snow. Her ears caught the rustle of a crusty oak leaf, moved by some tiny bird hiding in the underbrush. There was a feeling in the air of a season about to change, but for once Franny was not ready. Time was the enemy.

She could see the roof and jutting dormers of the Websters' neat house over the hill. Alice Faye and Charles would be waiting for her to walk to school with them. Shifting the bag of books, she tramped on, determined to meet the day a step at a time.

No one was outside, so she walked around to the side door and knocked. After a minute, Mrs. Webster poked her head out, saw her, and turned away quickly, putting her hand across her face—early-morning pale without her makeup.

"Alice Faye! Franny is here already. Hurry up!"

Without speaking to Franny, she closed the door again. Mrs. Webster was a very particular lady—not the sort who liked neighbors to see her in her nightgown.

Charles came out first, while Alice Faye scrambled around, yelling for her misplaced possessions.

"Monday mornings are always hard for Alice Faye," Charles said, his dark eyebrows drawing together thoughtfully.

Franny nodded. Alice Faye was as different as possible from her thin eighth-grade brother, who kept track of everything with unusual precision. He was sure to be valedictorian of his class.

"I've got some bad news." Franny decided to tell Charles first, because if Alice Faye came out babbling about something, there might never be a chance. "Mr. Copper told my papa he won't need him this year."

Franny was surprised to see alarm in Charles's dark eyes. "You mean you have to move?" he asked.

Before Franny could answer, Alice Faye came bursting out of the door, still struggling with her white rabbit-fur mittens. Only half her buttons were fastened, and her blond curls were sticking out haphazardly from her cap.

"Take it easy," Charles said. "We still have sixteen minutes—we can wait for you."

"I *had* everything ready," Alice Faye explained, "but then my hairbrush was missing, and I had to look for it, and Mama takes *forever* to brush my hair. . . ."

"Franny has to move," Charles said.

The look on Alice Faye's round face was one of shock. She seemed ready to faint or cry, so Franny hurried to explain.

"What I said is that Mr. Copper won't hire my papa again. He said we could stay in the house."

Alice Faye let out a sigh of relief, but Charles looked puzzled.

"I don't get it," he said. "I thought he really liked your father."

"All I know," Franny said, "is that he went to Milwaukee and came back with another hired man. I s'pose his wife told him to. She always bosses him."

Charles needed a logical explanation for everything. "Why would she do a thing like that? Your father was doing a good job."

Everything suddenly seemed crystal clear to Franny. "I think it's because she doesn't like my mama," she said. "She was always coming over, bragging about her married daughters, how they put up so many jars of preserves and sewed all their own clothes, and worked in the fields besides. My mama's family always had a housekeeper—she can't do any of that stuff."

"Neither can mine," Alice Faye said.

"But your mama doesn't *have* to. She can afford store-bought things."

"So can Mrs. Copper, I'll bet," Charles said.

"How do you know?" Alice Faye asked. It was strange how Alice Faye, who believed anything Franny told her, always challenged her brainy brother.

"Because they own their farm," Charles explained patiently. "They aren't in debt, so they have money even when times are bad. It's the people with debts who can't make it."

"And people without jobs," Franny added.

"Don't worry, Franny. Your dad will find something. He has a good reputation around here." It was hard to believe that Charles, who sometimes put on superior airs, was being so nice.

"Maybe Papa could give him a job," Alice Faye suggested.

Charles frowned. "I doubt that," he said. "Nobody is buying much building material now, either. I'll ask him, though."

"That darn Mrs. Copper," Alice Faye said, and linked her arm through Franny's as they walked.

It was hard to concentrate on schoolwork that day, for every time there was a lull, the worries all closed in again. The more Franny thought about it, the more certain it seemed that Mrs. Copper was the one responsible. A daring idea was forming in her mind—maybe it was not too late to make her change her mind. Franny had never known anyone to argue with Mrs. Copper, but there was always a first time. What did she have to lose?

That afternoon, Alice Faye invited Franny to stop at their house on the way home, but Franny made an excuse and hurried on toward the thicket. She didn't feel like telling Alice Faye her plan. Besides, Papa wouldn't like it, and just this once she was going to do it, anyway.

From the thicket she sneaked around toward the woods west of the house and, hidden by trees, made her way down to the road without being seen. From there, it was no time at all until she found herself on the back porch of the Coppers' large, sturdy farmhouse, knocking bravely on the door.

Just for a second, Franny hoped no one was home, or that they hadn't heard her. But Jack had sharp ears and came dashing from behind the sheds, yelping his welcome. At the same time, she could hear heavy footsteps coming toward the door.

"Shut up, Jack!" Mrs. Copper shouted before she even opened the door. When she saw Franny, she looked surprised.

"Well! The little Parsons girl! Why aren't you in school?"

"I just got home—it's almost four." Franny was annoyed at the question, because it made her forget what she wanted to say. "May I come in for a minute?"

"Why, sure." Mrs. Copper shook her large hand at

the dog. "Now get away, Jack, and stop that yappin'."

Franny found herself standing in the big kitchen, feeling like a tiny leaf in the linoleum pattern.

"I came to ask you to give my papa his job back." The words came out of her mouth, but it seemed some person much braver than she was saying them. Franny kept her eyes riveted on the starched apron bib that encased Mrs. Copper's front like a tarp over a haystack, and braced herself just in case one of those immense arms swung out at her.

Mrs. Copper gave a sort of muffled snort, and Franny's eyes slowly dared to travel up the leathery neck, past the prominent three-layer chin, a mouth that could not seem to decide whether to open or close, and on up to her eyes. She had never noticed Mrs. Copper's eyes before. Set deep beyond fleshy lids and scrubby lashes were these surprising little green circles, and right now they were staring at her as though she were Mrs. Copper's own little girl.

"Honey, I wouldn't hurt you for the world," she said, her gravelly voice trailing into a sigh. "It's a long story, but maybe I better tell you. Sit down here at the kitchen table and I'll get you a glass of milk."

This was not what Franny had expected. She perched stiffly on the edge of a heavy oak chair. Mrs. Copper got milk from the icebox, and her big hand brought out half a dozen molasses cookies from the depths of a tin can. Franny looked away. She hadn't come for cookies.

The big woman put the milk on the table and lowered

herself carefully into a chair across from Franny. "I s'pose they sent you so we'd feel sorry for you and change our minds," she said gruffly.

Franny flushed. "Nobody sent me," she said. "My papa would skin me alive if he knew I was here. I just think you're the one to blame, that's all."

"Why're you blamin' me?" Her voice was not unkind, but the green eyes were piercing.

"My papa was doing a good job for you. Everybody said so. Your husband said so. I know *he* wouldn't go and get somebody else. Unless you told him to."

"Then you don't know about Smokey?"

"Who's Smokey?"

Mrs. Copper snorted again. "He's my husband's no-good nephew. He's the one we're stuck with just to keep him out of jail. *He's* the reason you nice people are out of a job."

"Out of jail?"

"Oh, well, he's not dangerous or anything. Just a Milwaukee street loafer. Twenty years old and don't know any better than to steal a car. They were goin' to put him in jail—until his mama comes cryin' to my Carl. That's what she's done all her life—cries to get her own way. That's the reason she's got a no-good son, I'd say. But believe me, she wouldn't have got anywhere cryin' to *me*. It was Carl said we had to do it. *I* said six months in jail might straighten him out. But the judge let him off on condition he'd come to work for us."

"Oh." Suddenly Franny felt very embarrassed. She

should have listened to her papa. She pushed the milk away, untouched.

"I'm sorry, Mrs. Copper. I shouldn't have come."

Mrs. Copper pushed the milk back at her. "Sure you should," she said. "You should have come a long time ago, and you can come anytime you like. I miss having a little girl around the house. I spent so many years raising daughters—teaching them how to cook and sew and clean, and do their lessons and everything else a woman needs to learn—sometimes I think I taught 'em too well. They're so good at everything, they don't need *me* anymore."

Franny could hardly believe her ears. This big, tough lady was feeling sorry for herself. Just like anybody else. Hesitantly she reached out and took a cookie. She smiled and Mrs. Copper smiled back.

CHAPTER 4

Weathering the Storm

Every day was the same now. Papa was up early, ready to make the rounds again, checking every farm and village in the whole county for work. Mr. Webster had promised to keep his ears open for word of any jobs, and Julia Jarvis, the community nurse who had been such a special friend to them, made inquiries, but each day brought the same discouraging news. Nothing.

And all the while, that Smokey Manning strutted around the Copper farm as though he owned it, not even aware of how ridiculous he looked, fumbling through chores that any twelve-year-old farm boy could do with ease. And from the number of times the car whizzed up the road (nothing like the way Mr. Copper drove), he seemed to be finding all sorts of excuses to go to town.

Franny and Alice Faye saw him there one afternoon when Mrs. Webster had sent them on an after-school errand to Benson's Drugstore.

"Look who's sitting by the soda fountain pretending to be Clark Gable," Alice Faye whispered as they came in the door.

His back was toward them, but they could see his reflection in the mirror behind the malt mixer. Leaning forward slightly, he was flirting through his dark, half-lowered eyelashes with Peggy Ann Green, the waitress. Her cheeks were flushed and she kept dropping things.

"He better not let Peggy Ann's boyfriend catch him," Franny said. "Johnny Scholz could beat him with one hand tied behind."

"How come he wears those dumb clothes?" Alice Faye asked. "That suit coat looks like it came from the rag bag, and that V-neck sweater under it—" Alice Faye covered a fit of giggles with both hands.

"I s'pose he thinks it looks citified," Franny said. "And did you notice how he never wears a cap, even when he's working?"

"It might mess up his hair." Alice Faye giggled.

Right on cue, he reached into his breast pocket and pulled out a comb and pulled it carefully through his dark waves, right there at the soda fountain. He replaced the comb and took from the same pocket a cloth bag and cigarette papers. With skillful fingers, he shook tobacco onto a paper, rolled a neat cigarette, and placed it loosely in the corner of his mouth. Then he put away the makings and brought out a book of matches.

You'd have thought Peggy Ann was at the theater, the way she watched his performance. He stood up slowly and lit the cigarette. When he was ready to leave, he turned, looked back, winked, and blew a smoke ring at her. Then he sauntered out the door.

The two girls had kept out of sight behind a rack of hot-water bottles, but as soon as he was gone, they made their purchase and climbed up on stools right where Smokey had been. Alice Faye had two nickels, so they each ordered a root beer.

"Was that your new boyfriend?" Alice Faye asked innocently when Peggy Ann served them.

Peggy Ann blushed. "Of course not! I never saw him before."

"Well, that's good," Franny said firmly. "I've heard some pretty bad things about Smokey Manning."

"You have?" Peggy Ann looked shocked. "Like what?"

Franny bit her lip. She hadn't even told Alice Faye about Smokey's almost going to jail. "Just—stuff," she said.

"Well, he's sure good-looking." Peggy Ann glanced in the mirror behind the fountain. "Not that I'm interested—I'm engaged to Johnny Scholz, you know—but I'll bet some girls would like him."

Franny wrinkled up her nose. "I can hardly wait to see him on the manure spreader," she said.

She wouldn't have long to wait. The frost was beginning to go out of the ground, and in another month the fields would be ready for plowing. Only this year, Papa wouldn't be there to maneuver the team expertly while Mr. Copper used the tractor in another field.

At home, mealtimes weren't fun anymore. All Papa talked about was jobs. He'd heard that some big farms in Iowa might need workers. The TVA was building dams in North Carolina—maybe he would go there. Or maybe he would go back to Chicago and stand in line every morning for daywork like he had done before.

When he started talking like that, Mama's lips would tighten and Franny would start feeling scared. Unless a miracle happened soon, Papa was going to leave.

The last week in March, he stopped his daily trips. Instead, he stayed around the house, fixing things, checking the roof and the chimney, cleaning out ashes, and patching the screens that would soon be needed on the windows.

For two days he worked in the woods. He split up a huge oak that had crashed to the ground in the fall and hauled it behind Mr. Copper's team of horses to the yard. There was still a good-size woodpile behind the house, but he sawed and chopped the big oak slabs into usable pieces and stacked them neatly beside the others.

The potato bin in the cellar was almost empty, and he bought a hundred-pound sack from a farmer. On Saturday, he brought a big supply of groceries from town.

On Sunday morning, the family went to church as usual, but when they got home, Papa left the motor running. One by one, he hugged them and kissed them good-bye, gently loosening the hands that clung to him.

"You'll be fine, Rosie," he reassured Mama. Her face was pale and there were dark circles under her eyes, but she didn't cry.

Tears rolled down Martin's plump cheeks, and Franny, seeing him, nearly broke down bawling herself. She knew that would only make it worse. Later, when she was alone, she could cry, but right now she had to be brave.

"Franny, you're a strong, smart girl. Just try not to fly off the handle too often and help your mama all you can. You, too, Martin. And Sarah, be a good girl until Papa comes back."

"When?" Martin asked. "When will you be back?"

"It won't be long, son. I'm going to Chicago because I know that place best. I'm sure to find something there."

After another long embrace with Mama, he climbed into the truck, turned it around, and still waving, drove out of the yard and headed in the direction of the highway.

They lingered like shirts on a clothesline—limp,

empty bodies whose hearts had rattled on down the road with the man in the truck. Then slowly, silently, they trailed into the house.

The clouds had hung low all day, and by midafternoon, it was quite dark in the house. Mama lit a lamp and talked about the Sunday-school lesson, while Martin played with the blocks of scrap wood Papa had sanded down for him.

Franny tried to repeat what she had learned in Sunday school that morning, but after a few minutes, turned her head away.

"You're feeling bad, Franny," Mama said softly. "Maybe talking will help."

Franny searched for a way to start. "I—I've got this hard feeling inside of me, Mama—like I can't love God when He lets these bad things happen. I keep thinking He's forgotten me!" As soon as the words were out, she was frightened for having said them and reached out to Mama for reassurance.

The cool, dry hand hardly returned her squeeze. "Me, too," Mama said, looking off into space.

"Why is it so dark?" Martin asked. "Is it suppertime already?"

"It's going to storm soon," Franny explained, glad to change the subject. "The wind is getting stronger."

"It's making our house rattle," Martin said.

Mama seemed to notice that she had something else to worry about and shivered. "I hope no shingles blow off this time."

Martin carefully fit a block into place. "I'll fix them, Mama," he said staunchly.

The first distant thunder crashed, and soon lightning began flashing across the sky. Every rumble became louder, and the now-howling wind drove spikes of icy rain against the siding. The lamp flickered from the draft, and the trees outside the window swayed and creaked. Franny had never been afraid of storms, but without Papa here to protect them, she felt all quivery inside.

Even Sarah sensed the danger and whimpered until Mama picked her up. Quietly, Martin left his blocks and cuddled against Franny.

A brilliant flash and a terrifying explosion of thunder made them all jump. Franny ran to the window to see if a tree had been struck. All she could see was bending branches and more flashes. As the lightning continued its relentless slicing, they gave up pretending to be brave and huddled together, the four of them, all shivering. Again and again, the gusts of wind tore at the flimsy walls and a piece of roofing paper sailed across the yard.

Suddenly Mama tilted her head and held up her hand. "Listen!" she said. "I think I hear a fire siren!"

They all listened as its eerie wavering rose and fell through the noise of the storm.

"It could be in town," Franny said, "but it sounds more like it's coming around the bluff."

They dared to look out the window again, as bolt after bolt split the sky. The siren got louder, and as it passed the driveway, they could see the red flashing lights of a fire truck.

"Something's on fire!" Martin cried.

The woods to the west of their house blocked the view, but after the truck had passed, a red glow reflected in the low-hanging clouds above the trees.

"Oh, my God!" Mama stood holding Sarah, rocking back and forth, her eyes panicky.

"If the woods are on fire," Franny said, trying to keep her voice from trembling, "we'll have to get out of here. We could always go out the back way and over to Websters'. Those gusts of wind could send it in our direction. Let's wait and see. . . ."

They watched as the red glow spread higher above the trees. Then slowly, gradually, it grew fainter and finally disappeared from view.

"I bet the firemen put it out," Martin said. The storm was passing and the thunder had lost its edge.

"Or else the rain did," Franny added, for the rain had turned from sleet to a dense downpour. Already they could hear trickles coming through the attic—before long they'd have to set pans to catch the leaks.

About an hour later, the fire truck roared back toward Fisher's Glen. Shortly afterward, a car swerved into the driveway and squealed to a stop near the door.

"That's Coppers' car," Martin announced. "But they're sure driving funny."

Mrs. Copper lifted herself out on the passenger side and walked the few steps to the door. She was carrying something. Franny opened the door and waited while she wiped her sturdy shoes carefully before coming in.

"Well, I suppose you heard all the excitement," she said loudly.

"What happened?" asked everyone together.

"Lightning struck the tin roof on our corncrib. We had lightning rods on both ends, but that never stopped it. It went right through the roof and started it afire. The whole thing burnt down before the fire truck got there!"

"How terrible," Mama said, but she didn't sound as though it really mattered a lot.

"We thought the woods were on fire," Franny said. "We were pretty scared for a while. I'm sorry you lost your corncrib."

"It could have been a lot worse." Mrs. Copper shifted her weight and Franny hurried to bring a chair for her. "There wasn't much corn left in it, and we kept it from spreading to the other buildings—that's the main thing." Her eyes studied the offered chair. Papa had nailed braces between the legs, but it still didn't look too sturdy.

"I guess I'd better not sit down," she decided. "I've got Smokey waitin' for me in the car. I just got thinkin' about you folks alone up here and wondered if you had any damage. I see a few branches down in your yard."

"The roof is leaking a little," Mama said. "I guess some roofing must have blown off."

"I'll send Smokey over to fix it the first thing tomorrow. Carl's had the boy really working. He don't know much, but he learns real fast." Mrs. Copper set the package she was carrying on the table. "Chicken left over from dinner," she explained. "We've had so much excitement we ain't got much appetite for supper. You might as well have it."

As soon as the Coppers' car had gone careening out of the yard, Franny ripped open the package of chicken and could not help smiling. Leftovers, indeed! There was enough to feed them for three days—even with Martin's big appetite for his favorite food.

"I'll heat up some for our supper," Mama said, and then stopped in her tracks. She stared at the cookstove. They had forgotten it, and the fire had gone out.

"Your papa showed me how to start it," she began, "but I don't think I can do it. . . ." her voice trailed off.

"I've seen him do it a million times," Franny said impatiently. "I'll start it. I *hate* cold chicken."

Mama looked at her sharply. "Of course you won't, Franny. You're not old enough to start a fire. I'll manage."

Franny went to the woodshed and poured a little kerosene from the can into a tin cup, like Papa always did. She picked up a few dry corncobs and took them to her mother. There was dry wood in the woodbox next to the stove, and Mama made an awkward arrangement of cobs and wood. Fearfully, she dribbled the kerosene over it and retreated to the far end of the kitchen.

Crouching, she slowly approached the stove again, match in one hand, ready to strike against the side of the box. Four feet from the stove, she suddenly lit the match and flung it, in a single wild motion. It glanced off the stove and fell to the floor. Franny walked over and stepped on it.

"Now, get back, Franny! I'll get it this time!" Again Mama came creeping with the matches, and this time her aim was better. Flames flared toward the ceiling and then subsided to a steady crackle.

Triumphantly Mama slammed down the iron lid, as though she had captured a tiger. In no time at all, they were enjoying hot chicken.

CHAPTER 5

The Planting Season

The thunderstorm brought spring to the Wisconsin countryside. Brand new leaf buds were bulging and the sun-warmed earth steamed with rich aromas. Smokey Manning showed up very early Monday morning with a ladder and toolbox. He came to the door just as Mama was going through her ordeal of lighting the fire.

"Oh, here—let me do that for you, ma'am," he offered, stepping inside without being invited. He took the matches out of her hand and started the blaze with no fuss at all, just as Papa would have done. Then he looked at Mama carefully, with a polite smile.

"I'd be glad to come over and start that for you every morning if you'd like," he said.

Mama looked so frail and helpless, standing by the window with the sun picking up highlights in her long hair. Just like a lady in a storybook, waiting to be rescued.

Franny stepped in front of her. "Thanks just the same," she said coldly. "We can start our own fire."

Smokey stared at her, surprised, and then looked toward Mama.

She nodded. "Yes—thanks just the same."

Smokey shrugged agreeably. "Guess I'll see what I can do about that roof now," he said. He took the comb out of his pocket and ran it through his wavy hair.

Martin and Franny tagged along to watch. Smokey didn't look as though he'd ever fixed a roof before. He almost fell getting off the ladder at the top, and then instead of striding the pitched roof as Papa would have, he crawled on his hands and knees, locating the holes.

There was one long piece of roofing gone, as well as several smaller pieces, and Franny snickered at the expression on his face when he realized that he had hammer and nails but had left the roll of roofing paper on the ground. He looked at the ladder and muttered a cussword under his breath. Coming down would be even harder than going up.

"I don't suppose you kids are big enough to help with this," he remarked.

"I don't suppose," Franny agreed.

Martin gaped at her. "We always helped Papa," he said.

"That was different. Anyway," Franny said, looking up at Smokey, "you don't expect us to carry that big roll of roofing up the ladder, do you?"

"No, I guess not."

Martin had to put in his two cents again. "Franny could cut off a piece." She scowled at him and shook her head.

Smokey was suddenly smiling. "Well, now, that's a right good idea, sonny. The shears are right there in the toolbox, Toots. Cut me off a piece about—this—long."

Franny shot him a dirty look, but decided to do what he suggested. After all, the roof did need to be fixed. She cut all the strips he needed and climbed up the ladder with each one. He looked scared every time he came close to the edge for one, especially when she thrust it at him a little harder than necessary.

When all the holes were patched, he again looked dubiously at the ladder. He would have to turn around and back onto it.

"I'd ask you to hold that ladder steady for me, Toots, but I somehow get the idea you'd enjoy seeing me fall and break my neck."

Martin had gotten tired of watching and gone into the house by this time, and Franny decided to say what she was thinking.

"Sure, why not? Then my papa could have the job you stole from him."

His eyes narrowed as he looked down at her. "Yeah, I *thought* that was what you were sore about. Well, believe me, it wasn't *my* idea. He could have this job back in a minute if—" He decided not to finish the sentence.

"You mean it's as bad as jail?" Franny asked boldly.

"So Aunt Hazel blabbed about that, huh? Yeah, there's really not much difference, not with *her* for a warden. This way I get the hard labor, too."

"You prob'ly never did any before," Franny taunted. "Here, I'll hold your old ladder for you, just so you can *leave.*"

Cautiously, he made his way down the ladder, sighing with relief when he reached the ground. He picked up his toolbox.

"Tell your ma to let me know if there's anything else she needs done. She's a real pretty lady."

Franny threw her most evil-eye daggers at him and stalked into the house.

Two weeks passed before any word came from Papa, and then it was only a postcard from Chicago. The excitement of hearing from him was dampened by the familiar tone of the message—he hadn't found a job, other than a couple of days of odd jobs, "but something is sure to turn up soon." It was painful, learning to live without him, and seeing Smokey around made it all the more unbearable.

Mrs. Copper visited a couple of times a week, always bringing something—fresh-baked bread or a jar of applesauce or jelly. She told Mama how to control the fire in the cookstove and even showed her how to bake bread, but Mama just didn't seem to have a knack for it. She was always burning things, or else they weren't quite done in the middle.

After the health nurse, Julia Jarvis, stopped by with a batch of nutrition leaflets, Mama did learn to make a pretty good navy-bean soup. Martin and Franny sorted beans every Saturday afternoon, because if Julia Jarvis looked at you with her level gray eyes and said beans were good for you, you had to believe it.

She was a practical nurse—the nearest thing to a doctor that Fisher's Glen had. When Sarah was being born and Mama was scared half to death, it was Julia who took charge and calmed Mama down, and the first thing you know, there was Sarah, as pink and healthy as could be.

Julia seemed to know almost everything, except how to make her own son smart. Big Gil was in eighth grade, had flunked twice, and could hardly even read yet. Everybody said what a shame it was.

But Julia never let on that anything was wrong. In fact, she had taught him to drive and he chauffeured her on her rounds whenever he was out of school. Still, Franny could not help feeling sorry that this helpful, much-admired nurse should be burdened with a retarded son.

Julia was the one who reminded Mama to plant a garden, too. That was the first thing Papa had done a year ago, but Mama had no idea how to go about it. Mrs. Copper seemed delighted to be of use again.

"Smokey hasn't had no experience in the fields, so

Carl is letting him plow the gardens. Soon as he gets ours done, I'll have him plow yours. Then we can get busy and do the planting," she promised.

Sure enough, a day later, Smokey showed up with black Jupiter hitched to a stoneboat, on which rested the awkward walking plow. Mama went out to show him the garden plot.

"It's good of you to help," she said. "I hope I'll be able to raise some vegetables. My husband did it last year, but I don't know anything at all about gardening."

"To tell you the truth, it's all new to me, too." Smokey grinned at her as though they were sharing a secret. "This country life is really somethin', ain't it?" He unloaded the plow at one corner of the garden and hitched it to Jupiter's harness. Then, lowering the plowshare, he yelled a giddap at Jupiter and almost lost his footing when the blade tore into the soil.

"Look at him," Franny said to Mama as they watched him struggle to cut a steady furrow. "You can tell he never worked before. I bet we'll have a crooked garden this year."

Mama patted her shoulder. "Now, Franny, give him a chance. He's young and has a lot to learn yet."

"I just wish he'd learn it someplace else," she replied glumly.

Mama went back to the house, but Martin and Franny stayed to watch. On the second round, Smokey stopped the horse, tore off his jacket, and flung it to the grassy edge of the garden. His handsome face was twisted as though in pain, and damp tendrils of hair had fallen over his forehead.

"Watch him reach for his comb," Franny whispered, but this time she was wrong. He grimly unlashed the reins from the plow handles and continued his task, staggering up one furrow and down the next. It was not a large garden, but by the time he finished, he was flushed and panting.

He stopped in front of the children and, still breathing hard, forced a smug grin. He seemed about to say something to Franny, but changed his mind and spoke to Martin instead.

"Marty, how's about gettin' me a dipper of water? I sure am dry."

Martin stole a glance at his sister and then trotted off toward the well. She followed him. Martin tried to help with everything, but the pump handle was pretty stiff and he probably couldn't manage it alone. Besides, Franny did not relish the company of Mr. Smokey Manning.

They filled the gallon lard bucket and took it back to Smokey, who by this time had sat down on the grass to rest.

"Thanks, kids," he said, and took a long drink from the bucket. Sighing with satisfaction, he splashed some of the water on his hands and arms, and even on his face and neck. Then out came the comb, and a minute later he was looking just as perky as ever.

He took another drink and got to his feet.

"Hallelu!" he yelled. "We got that job done!" With a sudden swing of the bucket, he whipped the remaining icy water over Jupiter's back.

Squealing with alarm, Jupiter reared up on his hind legs and bolted toward the road. The plow, with no one to guide it, bounced crazily behind, panicking him even more.

"Dad blast it!" Smokey took off after the runaway while Martin and Franny stood frozen, watching.

Near the corner of the driveway stood a half-grown elm tree, and Jupiter swerved close to it, hoping to shake off the plow.

"He'll stop now," Franny whispered hopefully, as the plow caught on the tree. Jupiter only grew more excited, hurling himself about with rolling eyes, his open mouth fighting the bit.

"Whoa, there, Jupiter!" Smokey had almost reached the horse, when, with a mighty lunge, Jupiter tore free and sped toward the road. Trailing chains and broken harness, he headed for home.

Smokey stood looking at the mangled plow for a minute—too mad to even cuss. Then without looking back, he slunk down the road toward the Copper farm.

"Maybe now they'll fire him," Franny muttered. Martin didn't say anything at all.

CHAPTER 6

Tony

By the middle of May, there had been no more word from Papa. Every day when the mailman passed by, Mama's eyes looked worried. She had no explanation for his not writing. Franny had terrible visions of him lying in some tree-covered ravine under the wreckage of the truck, but never told anyone. Mama was probably imagining, too.

Still, the garden was growing and things were not going too badly. One day on the way home from school, Franny was halfway through the elderberry thicket when her nose picked up the aroma of fresh bread. Mama must have decided to try one more time!

Martin was waiting at the screen door, his eyes bright beneath his brown bangs. "We get a biscuit, Franny!" he said.

There they were, a pan of eight brown-crusted buns, and next to them three high loaves, a little lopsided, but otherwise perfect. Mama stood next to Sarah's chair, smiling.

"Well, I did it, Franny," she said. "I'm really learning to deal with that old stove." It was the first time she had looked happy for quite a while.

"They look yummy," Franny agreed. "May I have one?"

Mama nodded. "Put some jam on one for Martin, too. He's been waiting for you to come home. How was school today?"

"Same as usual. I'm glad tomorrow's Friday. After that, only two more weeks till vacation."

"When do *I* get to go to school?" asked Martin as his sister headed toward the pantry for jam.

"Not until a year from this fall," answered Franny. "But maybe you can come and visit someday."

"I don't think Martin's quite old enough," said Mama, the old uncertainty returning to her voice. From behind her, Franny gave Martin a wink and a nod. She knew Mama would give in.

They sat around the kitchen table and ate their biscuits. Mama had one, too, and broke off little pieces for Sarah, who stuffed them into her mouth greedily.

"Yoo-hoo!" came a far-off voice through the open window. "Yoo-hoo!"

"That must be Alice Faye," Mama said, smiling. "Isn't that your signal?"

"I'll be right back," said Franny, laying down her bread on the faded oilcloth. Outside she echoed loudly, "Yoo-hoo!" and a moment later saw her friend coming through the bushes toward her. Alice Faye had already changed out of her school dress into a blue slacks suit that had been "in fashion" last year. Alice Faye was both taller and plumper now, and the suit bulged at the buttonholes and showed the cuffs of her ankle socks. Wedged over her blond curls was a brand-new straw hat.

"Where'd you get the hat?" Franny asked.

Alice Faye's hands flew up to touch it proudly. "My aunt brought it for me," she said. "And guess what! My cousin's going to stay with us for the weekend."

"Which cousin?" Franny held her breath, hoping.

"My cousin *Tony*. You should see him. He's just finishing seventh grade and he knows how to dance, and he looks just like Mickey Rooney's friend in 'Strike Up the Band.'"

"I know—I saw him the last time he was here," said Franny, trying to sound casual. Tony was from Oak Park, Illinois, where all the boys were good-looking and stylish, according to Alice Faye. At least Tony was.

"Charles took him fishing and they won't be back till suppertime, but I think he's going to visit school with Charles tomorrow. Come over early and you can walk to school with us."

"I'll bet Dorothea Davis will be glad to see him." Franny wrinkled up her nose.

Alice Faye giggled. "The last time he was here she was making goo-goo eyes."

"And she's even *worse* now. Seventh-grade show-off!"

" 'Course she *is* pretty. Tony asked about her."

Franny sniffed. "Boys are really dumb," she said. "Come in and have a biscuit."

Alice Faye did not visit often. Mrs. Webster usually insisted that the girls play at her house. When Alice Faye did come, though, she never wanted to leave. Franny could not understand why she would like this rickety old house, with its makeshift furniture. The Webster house was all modern and everything matched. They even had a bathroom, and everyone knew Alice Faye's parents spoiled her rotten. Yet when she came to the Parsonses', she made herself right at home, answering Martin's endless questions, cuddling and playing peekaboo with Sarah.

At five o'clock she was in the rocking chair, her arms wrapped around little Sarah, while Martin rocked them.

"Isn't this the time you are supposed to go home?" Mama asked gently.

"No," she said, her blue eyes evasive. "Mama said I can stay a little longer today." She went on rocking.

It was going on six and Franny was already setting the table for supper when they heard Alice Faye's name being called. Quickly giving the little ones a final hug, she turned toward the door.

"Come out with me, Franny," she said. "It's Charles and Tony."

Franny gave Mama a quick glance, and she nodded. She had heard the news of Tony's visit by this time.

There he was, almost as tall as Charles, but more compactly built, sandy hair lacquered into a wave that just dipped a bit over his forehead, shading mischievous eyes. And of course, that confident tilt to his chin that Franny remembered so well. His pale, striped shirt, although faded, still looked stylish with its open collar, sleeves rolled just below the elbow, and tails neatly tucked inside his pants. He was wearing white tennis shoes. Nobody in Fisher's Glen wore white tennis shoes.

"Alice Faye, you're gonna get it from Ma!" Charles warned as the boys stepped out of the elderberry thicket. "You were s'posed to be home at five o'clock!"

"I was helping Franny baby-sit," Alice Faye explained.

"Isn't her mother home?" the older brother asked suspiciously.

"Well, yes, but—"

Tony broke in with a laugh. "Hey, don't give her a hard time, Charlie. Leave that to Aunt Mae. Hi, Franny. Long time no see. I think you're six inches taller than you were last year."

Franny could feel her cheeks burning, but she tilted up her nose a little and tried to look grown-up. "So are you. How come you're here? Is your school out already?"

He shook his head. "No, but I won't be coming this summer 'cause I'm going to summer camp. My folks had to go on a business trip and decided to let me stay here till Sunday night."

"He's coming to school with me tomorrow," Charles said proudly.

"I s'pose you can't wait to see Dorothea Davis." Franny hadn't intended to say that, but the words slipped out, so she looked him straight in the eye.

Tony suddenly made a big production out of rerolling his shirt sleeve, but recovered quickly and grinned back. "There has to be *some* reason to come to this hick town."

"Tell him about the list, Franny," Alice Faye said shyly.

"I don't think he'd want to know about *that,*" Franny replied doubtfully.

"What list?" His curiosity was aroused.

Franny looked down piously. "I never really saw it. They just talk around school about this list Dorothea keeps, numbered one through ten."

"Well, what's on the list?" Tony demanded.

Franny turned to Charles. "You tell him, Charles. You've prob'ly been on it already." Actually, it was very unlikely that a skinny bookworm like Charles would have been on Dorothea's list—if there even *was* a list.

Leaving Charles to his embarrassed denial, Franny decided she had said enough. "I've got to go. 'Bye, Alice Faye. See all of you tomorrow."

And she ran, barefoot, back to the house, where Mama was already dishing food on Martin's plate, while the place at the end of the table—Papa's place—was still conspicuously empty.

CHAPTER 7

The Prize

The schoolhouse was a big, square brick building on two acres of land, two blocks south of Main Street in Fisher's Glen. It held four classrooms, with two grades in each, plus a small library filled with every crumbling volume ever donated, regardless of subject, and a musty basement gym used only in bad weather.

Franny and Alice Faye were in sixth grade, and Charles would graduate from eighth in two weeks. Next fall, he would be going to high school over in Longfield.

Franny got up early so she would be sure to be in time to walk to school with the Websters and Tony. The boys walked ahead, but Franny and Alice Faye eavesdropped so they could repeat everything Tony said, when they met their other friends at school. Tony had brought his baseball and glove, and every once in a while, he would whirl around and, with a lightning-fast windup, pretend to hurl the ball toward them. He made them duck every time.

Kids were hanging around in clusters in the schoolyard, waiting for the bell to ring. Dorothea was nowhere in sight. Tony was looking around for her, although he tried not to let on. It was too late to start a ball game, so he just strolled around, tossing the baseball behind him and whirling to catch it, exchanging wisecracks with some of Charles's friends he had met before. Still no Dorothea.

At last the bell rang—its loud gong sending everyone hurrying into the building. Franny and Alice Faye waited at the end of the line. Just after Charles and Tony went in with the other seventh and eighth graders, Dorothea appeared, stepping out of her parents' shiny blue Buick.

Some of the seventh-grade girls had been talking about her habit of coming in a little bit late every morning, just so she'd be noticed. Not that she would have needed to do that. The way she tossed her dark curls over her shoulder, her glittering eyes, the inviting smile—even the way she walked—guaranteed that Dorothea would always be noticed.

Franny and Alice Faye made their own late entrance into Room 5-6, but the only notice *they* got was Miss Snyder's snappish "You girls had better get in here on time after this."

They could hardly wait for morning recess. There was no doubt that Dorothea would succeed in recaptivating Tony, but it would be interesting to see how she did it.

Maybe we'll learn something, Franny thought. *After all, that's what school is for.*

When the bell rang, she and Alice Faye were the first ones out the door, positioning themselves where they could easily move in the direction of the action. Dorothea came out with a group of other seventh-grade girls, chattering and laughing. They walked slowly to the shady side of the school and sat in a circle on a grassy knoll. Franny and Alice Faye and a couple of other classmates found a spot in the same area.

It was not long before Charles and Tony came in that direction. Very casually, of course—Tony still tossing the baseball from hand to hand. Dorothea had her back to him, and the boys had to circle around up the knoll in order to "accidentally" face her on the way back down.

Tony paused abruptly, as though catching sight of a familiar face. "Hi, Dorothea," he said, with his most charming smile. "Long time no see."

Dorothea seemed startled. She drew her eyebrows together, glanced questioningly at her friends, then back at Tony. "Do I know you?" she asked slowly. Then with a glimmer of recognition, but no enthusiasm, "Oh, yes. Charles Webster's cousin. Hello."

As though her social duty had been accomplished, she turned her head and began talking to her friends.

Dorothea's attitude was unbelievable! Last summer, she had kept Tony going in circles with her flirting. Now she seemed completely uninterested, leaving him to stand red faced, struggling to retain his self-assurance. Tossing the baseball behind him, he whirled to catch it, and he and Charles walked off toward the game on the baseball diamond.

As soon as he had left, Dorothea smiled broadly at her friends, and they all burst into giggles.

Recess was over quickly, but lunch hour was longer. Surely something would happen then. Franny and Alice Faye started outside with their lunch boxes. Dorothea was next to them, going down the cement steps. Just behind her was Gil Jarvis, Julia's son, dull faced and dressed in bib overalls. Gil was fifteen and a head taller than most of the eighth-grade boys. When a sudden surge of students coming out the door sent everyone pushing, it was big-boned Gil who lost his balance and stumbled forward against Dorothea. She half fell, grabbing the railing at the last minute, screaming.

Recovering herself, she turned to Gil, her eyes flashing. "You big, clumsy ox! Watch who you're pushing!"

Gil was plainly mortified. He always tried to avoid attention, perhaps because being noticed often meant being teased. So far as Franny knew, it was not in his nature to cause trouble deliberately.

"I didn't mean to," he mumbled.

Dorothea snorted in disgust.

Glancing behind her, Franny saw Tony at the top of

the stairs, his mouth set in an angry scowl. He had seen what happened. For a second he hesitated. Then, with the grace of a cat, he threaded his way through the crowd on the steps and confronted Gil, who was trying to move away. Tony's fists were doubled and poised for fighting. His voice was tough.

"Hey, bully, what's the idea of pushing girls?"

Gil shook his head, agitated. "N-no. I *didn't.* No."

"What do you mean, you didn't? I saw the whole thing. You tried to push Dorothea down the stairs!"

"N-no. It was—an accident." Gil was twitching nervously, biting at his lips.

"Don't give me that crap." Tony was working up to something. Everyone was watching, and like an actor on a stage, he drew confidence from his audience.

"I'm not going to stand here and watch you get away with what you did," he continued, jabbing one of the fists into Gil's ribs. "We're going behind the school and you can show *me* what a tough guy you are."

"I never did what you said," blustered Gil, his face flushed. "But I can show you . . ." He flailed out with one raw-boned arm.

That was what Tony had been waiting for. Like a boxer he tore into the bigger boy, his knuckles landing a solid volley about the chest and shoulders. Gil tried to punch, but Tony dodged and ducked. It was like a wolverine battling a moose. Gil's blows continued to miss their mark, and he began breathing hard, using his hands to protect himself from Tony's barrage.

Tony's footwork had gradually moved them around to the side of the building, and some of the kids were shouting encouragement. From the first, Franny had been shocked and frightened at what she saw. She had always avoided Gil as much as anyone, but now for some reason, the blows that were punishing his ungainly body seemed also to land in the pit of her stomach.

She looked around. Charles was shoving one fist into the palm of his other hand in rhythm with each of Tony's punches. The boys, who were cheering, were all plainly on Tony's side. There was a kind of excited glaze over the eyes of some. Even Alice Faye was spellbound.

And there was Dorothea. She was leaning forward, her lips parted in a half-smile, her eyes shining. The battle was for her, and she was the prize. It was plain that Tony would be rewarded.

"We've got to get a teacher!" cried Franny.

One of the eighth graders pushed her. "Shut up, tattletale," he said.

Gil was puffing loudly now, his shoulders bent low to ward off Tony's nonstop assault. Tony saw his chance—Gil's curly head was within his reach. He sprang with an upward blow, catching Gil's cheek, and before the big boy could recover, he was back with another to the nose. It made a sickening, cracking sound, and blood spurted out.

A few people gasped and someone said, "Gil bleeds easy."

Like an enraged bull, Gil lunged blindly. "Damn you!" he shouted.

Tony danced away and turned a triumphant face to the crowd, then moved in and struck two more blows to Gil's suffering face. Gil staggered and almost fell. With a muffled whimper, he covered his face with his hands. Blood was everywhere. He turned his big body away and stumbled off toward the street. Half-stifled sobs escaped him, and Franny felt sick.

Tony stood still, out of breath and sweaty now, too, his hair tousled and his hands bloody. Still, he managed to smile and with a shrug, moved over to the water faucet on the side of the school.

Dorothea was there, offering him her handkerchief. "You sure can fight," she said.

"Only when I *have* to," Tony said modestly.

Alice Faye pulled at Franny's sleeve. "Where should we sit to eat our lunch?" she asked.

Franny looked down the street, where Gil was lumbering toward home, then back at Alice Faye. "You can have mine," she said.

The excitement was over. Everyone else seemed ready to forget it and go on with the day. Only Franny couldn't do that. The afternoon seemed endless; she could hardly concentrate on her schoolwork.

In her mind was this confusing question, for which there was no answer. Although she had never admitted it to Alice Faye, Tony had been her idol since the first time she saw him. Gil, on the other hand, was just a big dummy. So how come she had kept hoping that Gil would win the fight?

There was no one to talk to about it and she couldn't bear the thought of walking home with Tony and the Websters. She told Miss Snyder she had a bad stomachache and left early.

Mama was surprised to see her home so early and asked what was wrong, but Franny wasn't ready to talk to her, either.

"I don't feel good," she said, holding her forehead. "I'm going to lie down for a while."

She went to her room and lay on the cot, staring at the blistered brown paint. Closing her eyes, she could see the whole fight over again, and still there were no answers. There was only one person who could help sort it all out. If only Papa would come back.

CHAPTER 8

Second Chance

Franny stayed away from the Websters all weekend. Alice Faye came looking for her, but she
shook her head.

"I have to work," she said shortly. "And there's nothing you can help with."

It was true. There was always plenty of work to do,
and Alice Faye wouldn't have lasted an hour out in the
garden. The vegetables were growing fast, but the weeds
grew even faster. It took all morning to thin out the
carrots and hand-pull weeds from around the young
bean and tomato plants. Saturday afternoon, Franny
hoed the whole potato patch and went to bed that night
with a sunburned neck and blisters stinging both palms.

After Sunday school, Franny settled herself under the

silver-maple tree with the box of old sweaters Mrs. Copper had given them. Patiently she unraveled them and wound the yarn into balls. Even Martin helped a little, off and on. Mrs. Copper had promised to teach them how to knit. By winter, they should have plenty of warm mittens and socks—maybe even sweaters, if they got really good at it.

Still, it was easy to imagine what fun the Websters must be having with their houseguest. Franny hoped that Alice Faye wouldn't be mad at her for staying away. Alice Faye seldom held a grudge.

Sure enough, Monday morning she was chattering away as usual and it turned out that Franny hadn't missed much after all.

"They fished all Saturday afternoon in Papa's row-boat—Tony and Dorothea and Charles and Opal Johnson—and *then* they went to the drugstore and hung around till almost suppertime."

"Don't make it sound like I was with Opal Johnson," Charles objected. "She just came along with Dorothea."

"And how many fish did you catch?" Alice Faye taunted.

Charles blushed. "Those dumb girls made so much noise, they scared 'em all away."

Alice Faye hurried on. "—and then Saturday night Papa took us to the movie over in Longfield. I hated it—it was all about airplanes."

"An excellent movie," Charles said. " 'Flight from Glory.' "

"I hated it," Alice Faye repeated. "And then guess what! Sunday, Dorothea's family took Tony on a picnic, and by the time he got back, my aunt and uncle were here to pick him up."

"That wasn't very nice," Franny said, noticing Charles's scowl.

"I guess *Tony* thought it was," said Alice Faye. "He gave Dorothea his Boy Scout pin."

"Not really his Boy Scout pin," Charles muttered. "Just his old Cub Scout pin. No use keeping that."

The fight with Gil Jarvis was never mentioned, but the memory of it still simmered like molten lava inside Franny. At recess, the word was passed around that Gil was absent and wouldn't be coming back to school at all. His mother was going to teach him at home.

"He's really a poor loser," Alice Faye said, walking home that afternoon. "He didn't have anything to be afraid of—Tony's gone now."

The hot lava bubbled up. "It's more than that!" Franny snapped. "It's a *lot* more than that. I don't blame Gil for hating this whole rotten school."

Alice Faye's blue eyes flew wide open with surprise, but Charles, who had been scuffing along somberly, got the message.

"Well, it wasn't *me* that did it, Franny."

Franny stared at him silently, and his face started getting red.

"Tony just didn't understand what Gil is like," he

said. "None of the guys from our school would have done that."

"Then why didn't you *tell* Tony? You could have stopped him."

Some muscles in Charles's chin were jiggling, and his eyes focused on a piece of gravel he was kicking along the roadside.

"There wasn't time," he said. "Nobody else was—" His chin jerked up suddenly. "All right, Miss Goody-Goody, how come *you* didn't?"

"Me? Who'd listen to me? I'm only—" Franny stopped, caught in her own trap. She hung her head, all the wind gone from her sails. "I don't know. I wish I had."

"Well, don't feel bad about it," Alice Faye said cheerfully. "Big kids are always getting in trouble. Gil will prob'ly learn more at home, anyway. His mother *likes* him."

Alice Faye could sure make everything sound simple.

As it turned out, it was nowhere near that simple. Julia Jarvis stopped in the next Saturday morning to see how Mama was doing with the nutritious foods she had recommended. At least that was the excuse she gave. Gil, as usual, waited behind the wheel of their well-kept four-year-old Chevy out in the driveway.

Franny was in the kitchen washing fresh lettuce and radishes—the garden's first produce—and took her time so she could listen in on the conversation.

There was something different about Julia today. Her slim, strong fingers kept picking at the edge of her notebook, and a couple of times she forgot—in the middle of a sentence—what she wanted to say about the value of vitamin A.

All at once she stopped and said what was really on her mind.

"Rosalyn, I need to ask your advice. I just don't know who to turn to."

Mama looked surprised, as though no one had ever asked her for advice before.

"It's Gil," Julia went on. "I'm sure you've heard of his problems with schoolwork, but for the first time I'm really worried about his future. Most people don't realize it, but Gil is really a bright boy. He can figure math problems in his head that I wouldn't even *try,* and other subjects, too. I've kept thinking sooner or later he would catch on. The school's never taught him to read, and that holds him back in everything. I want him to go to high school—even college. But after what happened last week, I've just given up on that school. I went to the school board and told them I was sure I could do a better job myself."

Franny wondered if Mama would ask what had happened last week, but she only said, "Oh, I'm sure you could, Julia."

Julia shook her head. She looked ready to cry. "I *can't.* It's like a brick wall. We read the same simple sentences until he has memorized them, but he still doesn't know those same words the next time he sees them. And what's worse"—her eyes filled with tears—"I've lost my temper. I've screamed at him. I even called him stupid! My own son, Rosalyn. And I can't even help him!" Her voice broke and she slumped in the straight kitchen chair.

Mama looked very sad, too, but her puzzled eyes made it plain she had no idea what to do about it.

Julia straightened up and cleared her throat. "I'm too close to him. I want so badly for him to succeed. That's why I lose my patience when he fails. That's no good. I wondered—would you work with him, Rosalyn? I'd be willing to pay—"

Franny could see that Mama was upset. Julia should have known better than to ask her something like that. Already she was shaking her head vigorously.

"No, no, not me. I couldn't! My husband is the reader in the family. If only he were here. He reads everything he can lay his hands on. And Franny's the same way—but of course she's only in sixth grade."

Julia slumped again. "I just don't know what to do," she said.

Franny stared down at the lettuce swimming crisply in its water bath, an idea forming in her mind. "Charles Webster is eighth-grade valedictorian," she said softly. "Maybe he could help."

Julia glared. "Oh, no, he couldn't. He's one of *them.*"

"But he's sorry about what happened. I know he is. Let me ask him," Franny urged.

"I doubt that would work. I'll try to think of something. . . ." With a sigh, Julia picked up her notebook and rose to her feet. "I'm glad your vegetables are coming now," she said in her clear, professional voice. "And keep up the bean soup."

"You're crazy, Franny," Charles said. "*Nobody* can teach Gil Jarvis to read, and I wouldn't even try."

"His mother says he's smarter than he looks. She says he figures math in his head."

It was Sunday, and Charles, in his white shirt and tie, his thin hair flattened with hair tonic, looked very superior.

"He may be trainable in some areas," he said stiffly, "but the fact is that the person of average intelligence learns to read in first grade."

Franny could see that she was getting nowhere, so she forced tears to her eyes by thinking very hard about Papa and adjusted her voice to a husky tremble. "We stood and watched that fight, Charles. Neither of us stuck up for Gil. I feel so ashamed. If we could just make it up to him—" One of the tears slipped out and rolled down her cheek.

"Now, don't start bawling," Charles said nervously. "Sure, I feel sorry for him, but that's not going to change the way he is. He's feebleminded, Franny, and that's that."

"Then you won't help at all?"

"It wouldn't be helping him, and it would just make

it bad for me if it got out that I was hanging around a dummy."

She should have known. The Websters always thought first about how they looked to others.

"Then I guess I'll have to do it myself," Franny said scornfully. She turned and walked briskly away from Charles. Gil Jarvis and his mother lived a mile away, on the other end of town, and that was where she was headed.

CHAPTER 9

Reaching Out

The first Monday in June, Julia dropped Gil off with his schoolbooks. Franny saw him coming toward the door, looking as though he were being pushed from behind, and didn't blame him a bit.

What have I gotten myself into? she thought. *I told Julia I'd help him until she could find someone else, but I sure hope she'll find someone soon.*

Mama greeted him politely and then busied herself with the housework.

"Uh—Gil—I see you brought your books," Franny said awkwardly.

He nodded, holding them stiffly. He was neatly dressed, and if his mouth had not been pressed into what seemed a permanent scowl, he would not have been bad looking. His gray eyes, fringed with dark lashes, shifted quickly away from Franny, and he bit his lip nervously.

"I s'pose we could sit by the table." Franny pushed a chair in his direction and they both sat.

Franny examined the books with dismay. They were thick eighth-grade books—science, civics, grammar.

"This stuff looks pretty hard," she said doubtfully, leafing through them. The pictures in the science book caught her attention.

"This looks interesting," she said, and turned to page one: How to Interpret Data—Planning an Experiment with Pendulums.

"Do you want to start here—just for practice?" she asked.

His thick eyebrows were pulled together and the corners of his mouth turned downward. He stared at the page and the silence seemed endless.

"Can you start?" Franny asked again.

"It's about pendulums and how they work," he mumbled in his deep, uneven voice.

"You can tell that from the pictures," Franny accused. "What does it say about pendulums?"

He continued to stare at the page. "I don't know," he said.

"The first word—in black print," she prompted.

He tried to form a word with his mouth, but wouldn't say it.

"This is a hard book," said Franny. "I have trouble reading it, too. If you wouldn't be insulted, why don't we use this old fourth reader I had when I was in Chicago? Would that be all right?"

Franny took it from the high shelf where she kept it since Sarah had started to walk. She opened it to the first story—"Androcles and the Lion"—and placed it in front of Gil.

He looked really miserable. He cracked his knuckles under the table. "I can't," he said.

"Just one word at a time," Franny coaxed. "If you get the first one, the rest are easy."

"An-another?"

"You're close. It's An-dro-cles. Okay. What's next?"

"Androcles"—he said the name carefully—"and—a lion!" He looked up hopefully.

"That's right, only it's *the* lion." Of course, the illustration had helped him.

Word by word they struggled through the story until it had lost all meaning. He had to be corrected on every other word. By the time they finished, Franny was really tired of it, but she figured since they had gone to all that work, she wanted to be sure he understood it.

"I'm going to read it straight through one more time," she said, and did.

"I've heard that before," he said when she finished.

It was enough for the first day. No wonder Julia was so upset.

The next day when he came, Franny asked him to read "Androcles and the Lion" again, hoping that he would do better now that he knew the story. He tried, but soon he was guessing and stumbling just as badly as he had the day before. He even mixed up easy little words like *was* and *saw*.

Mama suggested that they study for only ten minutes at a time and then take a ten-minute break. During the break, Gil crouched awkwardly on Papa's woodblock, searching the room with his dark eyes and cracking his knuckles loudly.

"How do you do that?" Martin asked.

Gil looked embarrassed and pulled his hands apart. "I'm not s'posed to," he said. "I forgot."

"Show *me* how," Martin begged, pushing at his own soft fingers, which didn't make any noise at all.

"I better not. Your mama wouldn't—like it," Gil said.

"Mama won't care. C'mon, show me!"

That Martin! Franny was a little embarrassed. He was too little to understand that there was anything wrong with Gil, and just set about making friends with him, with his shining eyes and endless questions.

Before long, Gil was smiling, answering Martin in a surprisingly smooth, low voice—more natural than the strained, choppy way he usually spoke.

Within the next two weeks, taking their cues from Martin, Franny and Mama treated Gil like one of the family, laughing and gently teasing, until he began to relax and they saw more and more flashes of his sunny personality.

They were surprised to find out that he loved jokes. He would tell Martin jokes he had heard on the radio, and after Mama and Franny encouraged him, he was soon sending them all into gales of laughter. He could imitate voices, and it was almost as good as hearing Charlie McCarthy or Fibber McGee themselves. They had missed hearing the programs since the batteries in their radio went dead.

Franny could see now what Julia had meant about his being bright. He was a different boy from the one she had seen at school.

Yet day after day when it was time to read, the sullen mask went on again, and the old, gruff voice made the same mistakes. It was Mama who discovered, just from listening, that some kinds of words were extra hard for him.

"I think you should just work on some of those hard words for a while, Franny," she said one day. "I'll print some cards with words that Gil can practice."

She cut up brown wrapping paper and printed some of the words that he most often read backward: *On, no. Saw, was. Top, pot. Bid, dip*—many others.

From then on, it was Mama who worked with those words. She made up little games like drawing boxes around words, to fit their shape. She let him trace words with his finger in the flour on her breadboard—so he could "feel" the shape of the words.

And Gil kept bravely stumbling through the fourth reader under Franny's faithful guidance. If nothing else, it took up some of the time she would have spent worrying why they still had no word from Papa.

Early in July, Mrs. Copper asked Franny to help her pick berries.

"The woods on Heddler's Bluff is loaded with raspberries," she said. "I like to put up a lot for sauce and jam, but my Carl won't let me go alone anymore, because of my—well—I need a spry picker. I'll give you five cents a bucket and all the berries you folks want."

"Can I, Mama?" Franny asked eagerly. She had been dying to explore the wild, spooky bluff for a long time, but Alice Faye was afraid of snakes and Mama wouldn't allow Franny to go alone.

"I don't see why not," said Mama slowly. "As long as it isn't during Gil's lesson time."

"I've got to get 'em in the morning," said Mrs. Copper. "By noon it's sweltering in the woods. I can't take the heat anymore."

Franny's face fell. Gil always came at eight and stayed until eleven. After that, he did yard work for several of Julia's patients.

Mama saw her disappointment and looked sad herself. She seemed about to say something, changed her mind, and turned away.

Franny was just about to tell Mrs. Copper how sorry

she was, when Mama decided to speak up after all.

"I guess maybe I could help Gil with his lessons—just for a few days, Franny. You go ahead and pick berries with Hazel."

CHAPTER 10

Berry Picking

Heddler's Bluff was just as exciting as Franny had imagined, as the two of them started out with their berry buckets. Mrs. Copper, in her straw hat and a huge pair of overalls pulled over her dress, took off like a plowhorse headed for pasture. She soon found an old wagon track left by woodsmen. It was so grown over that Franny would have missed it completely.

Mrs. Copper plodded right through the underbrush and low-hanging branches, apologizing when they snapped back, but never slowing her pace. It was all Franny's skinny legs could do to keep up, and she was glad she had worn overalls, too.

Within minutes, they were entirely out of sight of farms or road, swallowed up in the deep, mysterious forest. The dense foliage held back sounds from the outside world, and even when they spoke softly, their voices seemed very close and clear.

"How can you find your way?" Franny asked. "Don't you ever get lost?"

Mrs. Copper laughed good-naturedly. "I know this bluff like the back of my hand. I've been comin' here since I was younger than you."

"You mean you've lived in one place all your life?"

"You bet I have. My folks owned this farm, and my pa's folks before him. The bluff is county land, but we always come here for berries. Farther in we'll come to a spring—there's good watercress growing there. And in fall we gather hickory nuts—when we can beat the squirrels to 'em."

"And did your kids come up here with you, too?"

"Sure, they did. My girls had to learn early how to keep a family fed. I used to go out in the field and work right alongside my Carl in the summer. Makin' hay, fixin' fence—whatever needed doing."

"I s'pose if you'd had a boy, you wouldn't have had to do all that."

"We never complained. We was happy with what the Lord gave us." Mrs. Copper hesitated for a second. "'Course I have to say it's nice having Smokey around the place."

"Smokey!" Franny didn't bother to conceal the contempt in her voice. "You don't mean you're starting to *like* him. After all the dumb stuff he's pulled? He must have wrecked your harness when he plowed our garden."

Mrs. Copper chuckled. "I know—he's a greenhorn all right. But you've got to give it to him. He keeps right on tryin'. If he don't do something right the first time, he goes right back at it until he learns how. Every night he tells us how crazy we are to be farmin', but you know what? I've got a sneakin' suspicion he's startin' to like it himself. It's the first time in his life he's had a chance to be a man, and I think it makes him feel good."

"He sure seems awful anxious to run off to town every chance he gets," Franny said, but Mrs. Copper laughed that off, too.

"You can't blame him for that. A young fella needs a bit of fun now and then. He's turned out better than I expected, that's for sure."

Franny bit her lip. She didn't want to hear any more about Smokey Manning. He'd sure managed to pull the wool over Mrs. Copper's eyes.

They had been climbing in a steady upward direction, but now the path leveled out around the side of the bluff.

"There should be a good patch of berries just up ahead a ways," Mrs. Copper predicted, and was soon proved right.

The trees were not so thick here, and patches of sunlight reached the low bushes, ripening the luscious fruit. As they began picking, Franny savored the warm breeze on her skin and opened her nostrils to invite in the woody tree scents. The resentment she had felt a few minutes ago vanished, and she couldn't resist asking another question.

"Did *Mr.* Copper live near here, too?"

"He came from Hanesville—about thirty miles from here."

"How did you happen to meet him?"

Mrs. Copper chuckled again. "That was over forty years ago, girl. You expect me to remember that far back?"

"I'll bet you do!"

Mrs. Copper searched a branch for hidden berries, a little smile on her sunburned lips. "Well, see, Carl came from a big family. There were four boys—more than needed for their little farm—so he came to work for my pa as a hired man. By and by, my pa got too old to run the farm and sold it to Carl. And I was thrown in the deal."

Franny stopped picking and stared openmouthed at the older woman. "Not really!" she exclaimed.

Mrs. Copper just went on smiling and picking berries. It was plain that she didn't intend to give out any more personal information.

Their buckets were soon filled and it was time to start back. *Too soon,* thought Franny. She could not have imagined a more beautiful spot than this little garden set on the side of the bluff. Through the trees she could see the curve of the river that flowed past Fisher's Glen, and beyond it a collage of farm fields and woodlands. Picking up her pails, she reluctantly followed Mrs. Copper. What an easy way to earn ten cents.

By the time they took the berries to Mrs. Copper's kitchen and Franny returned home, Mama and Gil had finished the lesson and Gil was getting ready to leave.

"It went real well," Mama said after he was gone. "I just helped him with his words and then we tried another story in your book. I think he's improving, Franny."

"At least he tries," said Franny, shaking her head doubtfully.

"Yes, he does," Mama agreed. "And he's such a nice boy. Now that I know him better, I can see he's been covering up a lot of hurt."

Something in her voice surprised Franny. It was not like Mama to look beyond her own family for things to worry about.

The next day, Franny and Mrs. Copper finished picking the first berry patch and went on to another. As they walked, they could hear a trickle of water even before they saw the opening in the dark, massive rock where it came out. Below in a little gorge were thick, flowering masses of watercress.

"It's too late in the season for good watercress," explained Mrs. Copper. "Watercress is tastiest from fall to spring—even through the winter. You'll have to have some."

"We have lettuce in the garden now," said Franny,

"but I'll get some next fall." Would she still be here in the fall? She put the thought out of her mind and plunged on through the underbrush behind Mrs. Copper.

The footing became more treacherous as they moved higher on the bluff. There was no path at all, and rocks jutted out everywhere.

"Careful, watch your step," Mrs. Copper kept saying, but it was she, not Franny, who needed the warning. Her foot would land on an unexpected rock and at times her large body was hardly able to recover its balance. But she showed no sign of stopping—she was on her way to bring back raspberries.

When they finally reached the patch, it was even thicker with fruit than the first had been. The buckets were quickly filled and they made their way back—stopping short once to wait for a large spotted snake to get out of the way and be off on its own business, which did not take it long at all.

Mrs. Copper furnished the names of some unfamiliar plants—mandrake, fox grape, horse balm—and together they identified some of the birds.

On the third day, she left the leading up to Franny, who was proud to find enough landmarks to get all the way to the rocky spring and on to the berry patch. *Someday I would like to know this bluff like the back of my hand,* she thought.

They made good time that day, and when Franny reached home, she was surprised to see Mama and Gil standing side by side in the kitchen, reading aloud from the same book. Mama was holding a ruler to mark the line and putting her finger on each word as they pronounced it together—slowly, but with expression. Mama's voice was leading, but Gil was following better than he had ever done before.

When they finished the page, Mama was beaming. "Gil, that was very, very good!" she said. "Did you hear that, Franny? Didn't I tell you he's improving?"

"That was really good, Gil," Franny said, and he blushed with pleasure.

After he left, Mama explained that she had found out that Gil was actually seeing words and letters backward. He never knew which end of the word or line to begin at, and she was helping him set up landmarks on the page. That sounded pretty strange to Franny. After all, everybody sees the same thing, don't they?

It turned very hot overnight, and Mama thought Mrs. Copper might not want to pick berries the next day, but she came up the road with the buckets at eight o'clock, just like always. She didn't want those raspberries to go to waste.

Even that early, the woods were steamy and Franny's clothes stuck to her as she led the way up the bluff. They picked more slowly than usual, and Mrs. Copper often stopped to fan herself with a handkerchief. Franny was all sweaty, and deerflies buzzed around her ears. Picking berries had stopped being fun.

At last, the buckets were full and they started back.

There was no stopping to look at plants today. It would just be good to get home for a cool drink of water. Franny trudged along behind Mrs. Copper, watching ahead for the uneven rocks that could trip one so easily. Mrs. Copper was balancing herself on each side with a full bucket of berries, her shoes making an even *clomp, clomp, clomp* down the side of the bluff.

Even though the path was downhill, Mrs. Copper was panting, and her steps became gradually slower and less evenly spaced. A couple of times, she stopped and leaned against a scrub oak for a few minutes, mopping her face, which was flushed and dripping perspiration.

"I guess that's all the berry pickin' for this year," she said, as they reached the bottom. "I can't take this heat with my poor ticker. Anyway, we've got more than enough for both our families. I was going to make jam this afternoon, but now I think I'll have to sit for a spell with my feet in a cool pail of water."

"I'll help you make the jam," Franny offered.

Mrs. Copper considered that for a minute. "Maybe after supper, when it cools off a bit," she said. Then she got a better idea. "Say, why don't you ask your mama to bring the little ones and come, too. Then she can learn jam makin', as well as gettin' out for once. Seems she hardly ever goes anyplace."

"Papa always says she's not the sociable kind. But maybe she'll come this once. I'll ask her."

Gil had already finished his lessons when Franny came home. Martin and Sarah were outside, enjoying the piggyback rides he was giving them so much that they didn't want him to leave. Franny finally had to disentangle them from him.

"Mama says you're doing better every day," she told him. "I think she's a better teacher than I am."

He blushed and stared at his shoes like he always did when he was embarrassed. "She makes me feel like I can read everything, and then I *can.*" He quickly added, "But you help, too."

"We all want you to go to high school this fall."

Gil nodded. "I sure hope I can make it," he said.

The sound of a tortured engine and tires spitting gravel drew their attention to the road. The Coppers' car came roaring into the driveway, and Franny snatched up plump little Sarah, at the same time pushing Martin to safety near the house.

Smokey Manning brought the car to a screeching halt in plenty of time and sat grinning, his sun-bronzed elbow sticking jauntily out the rolled-down window.

Martin immediately escaped from his sister and ran toward the car.

"Howdy, old-timer," said Smokey as he reached out to grab Martin's hand.

"How come you drive so *fast?*" Martin asked. Admiration shone in his eyes.

"Fast? This ain't nuthin'. Sometime I'll take you for a ride and show you how fast this tin lizzie'll go!"

"Really?"

"No, I'm afraid not," Franny cut in. "Martin only

rides with people who know how to drive."

"Oh, is that right?" Smokey's eyebrows shot up. "Well, I guess I'd better learn how before seven o'clock, 'cause that's the time Aunt Hazel said to tell you I'd pick you all up tonight."

"We can walk just fine." Franny glared at him.

"I take my orders from Aunt Hazel," he retorted.

"Oh, that's right," Franny chided. "I forgot you had a jailer."

For the first time, Smokey lost his self-assurance and he looked embarrassed. "I've changed my mind about that," he mumbled. "Aunt Hazel's all right."

The next instant, he was smiling again and turned his attention to Gil, who stood shyly by.

"Hi. I'm Smokey Manning, and I guess you must be Gil. I'm real pleased to meetcha."

Gil mumbled a hello, but Smokey didn't seem to notice his awkwardness.

"I've seen you drivin' that little '34 Chevy around. Pretty flashy buggy. What's she got under the hood?"

"Gil's a *good* driver—not a maniac, like you," Franny interrupted. "Is that all you stopped for, to tell us what time—"

Smokey sighed and answered with exaggerated patience, "That's right—what time I'll pick you up. At seven o'clock. Be ready."

Then he turned friendly and relaxed again. "Say, Gil, do you need a lift downtown? I'm goin' that way—got to pick up some stuff at the feed mill. Hop in!"

To Franny's disgust, Gil hardly hesitated a second before accepting the invitation. He sprinted around to the passenger side, and off they went, at Smokey's reckless pace, looking like they'd been buddies forever.

CHAPTER 11

Raspberry Jam

Franny was still upset as she helped butter the bread and spoon out the bean soup for lunch, but she forced herself to put Smokey Manning out of her mind. Just as she had thought, it took a good bit of talking to get Mama to accept Mrs. Copper's invitation. There was no good reason why Mama wouldn't jump at the chance to go visiting, instead of spending another lonely night writing letters to Papa, when there was no address to send them to. But that was Mama's way—always had been—and Franny could hardly believe it when Mama finally agreed to go.

After lunch, Sarah and Martin were put down for long afternoon naps, and because it was too hot to do much else, Franny thought about visiting Alice Faye.

They had hardly seen each other since school let out. Even though Mrs. Webster was nice enough to Franny, she had dropped a few hints about the "influence of drifters." And some of Charles's comments about Gil Jarvis had sounded as though they could have come right out of his mother's mouth.

The Websters' attitude toward Gil still made Franny fume and was one of the reasons she had stayed away. *Not that Gil even cares whether I'm his friend or not,* thought Franny, remembering how eagerly he had gone off with Smokey Manning.

I think I will *go over to Alice Faye's,* she decided. *At least she doesn't like Smokey Manning.*

Alice Faye and her mother were on their screened porch. Alice Faye was arranging her large collection of dolls into happy little family groups. When she saw Franny, she pushed them aside, embarrassed at having been caught at such a childish pastime. Mrs. Webster, in a flowered sunsuit, reclined on a canvas deck chair, enjoying an electric fan, a sweating bottle of soda, and the latest *Collier's* magazine.

"Well, my word—it's Franny," Mrs. Webster said as Alice Faye unhooked the screen door. "We haven't seen you lately. I thought maybe you had moved away. Has your father come back yet?"

"No, he's still looking for work. He might be getting something real soon."

"I do hope so," sighed Mrs. Webster. "I wonder if

we'll ever see an end to these hard times. Thank goodness my husband is able to manage his business so well." She raised a plump hand, its nails carefully polished, patted her blond curls, then held it poised, ready to turn the page of her magazine.

"Alice Faye, honey, get a soda out of the fridge for you and Franny, and find a nice shady place to visit."

Alice Faye scooped her dolls into their wicker basket and led the way to the kitchen. "How come you haven't been over?" she asked.

"I've had work to do all summer," Franny explained. "Why didn't *you* come over?"

Alice Faye looked down and measured the cold soda carefully into two glasses. "I can't."

"Why not?" Franny asked sharply.

"I just can't, that's all."

"Is it because of Gil Jarvis? Is that why?" Franny wouldn't let Alice Faye off without an answer.

Alice Faye squirmed. "I guess so," she said. "Mama says you can never tell what'll happen around somebody like that."

"Like *what*? Why, isn't Gil just as good as you?"

"Well, look at how he pushed Dorothea down the school steps," she said defensively.

"Pushed Dorothea!" Franny could hardly believe her ears. "You were there, Alice Faye. You should know Gil never pushed Dorothea."

"Tony said he did."

"And Tony lies sometimes, too! My mama really likes Gil, and so do Martin and Sarah. He plays with them all the time."

Alice Faye looked hurt and tears filled her blue eyes. "It's not *my* fault," she said. "I want to come. I miss you. And I miss Martin and Sarah. Have they forgotten me?"

Franny's heart softened and she patted her friend's hand. "No, of course they haven't, Alice Faye. I'll bring them over someday. I promise."

Together the girls carried the cold drinks to the white painted lawn swing in the Websters' yard where they talked and giggled until it was time for Franny to leave.

As she walked back home through the woodsy thicket separating the end of town from her own yard, it occurred to Franny that she had forgotten to tell her mother that Smokey would be picking them up in the car. Or maybe she'd done it on purpose. She had been so mad about Gil going off with him that she couldn't stand to even say Smokey Manning's name again.

Now she was glad she hadn't. They could easily walk over a little early. Then maybe Mr. Smokey Manning would get the hint that they didn't want any favors from him.

Mama was peeling potatoes in the kitchen when Franny walked in, and Franny could tell she was worrying again.

"What took you so long, Franny?" she asked. "There's so much to do—Martin and Sarah need baths, and I have to make dinner. . . . What do you think I should wear, Franny? My housedresses are so faded—do you think my blue Sunday dress would be too dressy?"

"Yes." Franny tried to imitate the short, positive way Papa always answered when Mama was upset. "You're going to make jam—a clean housedress would be fine."

"You're right. But *clean.* Mrs. Copper is fussy about being clean. Do you think we'll all have time for baths? And my hair—is it all right?"

"I'll bring in the tub. There'll be time. And your hair looks nice." Mama's shining brown hair was always beautiful, even braided, as she wore it now because of the heat.

Franny brought in the galvanized washtub that hung outside the back door, set it up in the parlor, and added warm water from the cookstove reservoir. Martin let her bathe him quickly, but Sarah was at the age where she loved to splash, and Franny ended up almost as wet as her little sister. All the time she kept her eye on the clock. It was going to take careful timing to avoid Smokey.

Mama was so nervous, she hardly ate any of their simple supper and jumped up, ready to clear the table before the children were finished.

"Martin and I will wash the dishes," Franny volunteered. "You can start getting ready if you want."

Gratefully, Mama jumped up and headed toward the parlor with the teakettle.

"Mama's sure excited about making jam with Mrs. Copper," Franny whispered to Martin.

"Me, too," grinned Martin. "Will Smokey help?"

"I should *hope* not," Franny muttered, tossing her fork across her empty plate with a clatter. "Martin, I wish you'd keep quiet about Smokey!"

Her voice was sharp and angry. She knew she should stop, but the words kept coming out. "Don't you know it's Smokey's fault that Papa had to go away?"

Martin's mouth drooped and he stared at her, tears filling his big eyes. In a flash, Franny threw her arms around him.

"I'm sorry, I'm sorry, Martin. I didn't mean to yell at you." She knew it was wrong to take out her anger on Martin. Of course he was too little to understand. She tried to tease a smile from him, but she knew he would not forget so soon.

When the dishes were washed and dried, Franny headed for the parlor with the teakettle to warm up the bathwater and bathe as best she could. There was no way her long legs would fit in the tub anymore.

After putting on fresh clothes, she unbraided, brushed, and rebraided her pigtails, trying hard not to look at herself in the mirror. She was getting too old for pigtails, but it was the only way she could control her wild hair. Maybe Mama would let her get it cut before school started again, so she wouldn't be so ugly. Guiltily she thought of Papa, who had always loved her pigtails.

"I'm sorry, Papa," she whispered. "I won't be the same little girl when you come back. Some days I feel so much older. I'll be taller, and I might cut my hair, but

I won't ever—ever stop caring about you. And I promise to try harder to control my temper."

At last they were ready to go, and none too soon—it was almost ten to seven. Sarah, who had just started walking, would have to be carried. Franny looked at Mama, all fresh and cool looking. By the time she walked down the dusty road carrying chubby Sarah, she would be sweaty again.

Franny reached for her little sister and hoisted her to one shoulder. "I'll carry Sarah," she said. "C'mon, let's go."

Martin hung back, puzzled. "How come we're walking, Franny? Smokey said he'd pick us up in the car. Don't you remember?"

Mama turned to Franny, who felt herself flushing. How dumb could she be? Martin never missed anything.

"Did he—I mean—I thought he said—" she stammered.

"He said he'd pick us up at seven o'clock," repeated Martin.

Mama looked relieved. "Well, that's nice. Then we have plenty of time. Let's sit out on the grass and wait for him."

So they had to accept the ride after all. Smokey arrived right on time, and Franny silently herded Martin and Sarah into the backseat, letting Mama sit up front to engage in polite conversation with the driver.

"Do you have the milking done already?" asked Mama.

"No, but Uncle Carl let me off early. I figure on stopping over to see Gil Jarvis for a while, and then I'll be back in time to take you folks home again when you get done making jam."

"Oh, really?" Mama was surprised. "I didn't even know you knew Gil."

"Just met him today," said Smokey. "But we hit it off real well. I'd heard people talk about him some— y'know—saying how backward he is. But I don't think you can always judge somebody by a first impression. If you treat 'em right, you may find out they're not what you expected."

"That's just what my husband, James, always says," agreed Mama. "And Gil really is one who's worth it. We've come to know him real well this summer, and he's so different from the first time he came to our house. It's nice of you to take an interest in him, Mr. Manning."

"Just call me Smokey, ma'am. Well, see—to tell the truth—I can use a friend, too. Aunt Hazel and Uncle Carl are real good to me, but back in Milwaukee I always had a lot of friends. Out here I just don't seem to fit in yet. . . ."

Oh, sure. Tell some more lies. Make her feel sorry for you, thought Franny, watching her mother nodding sympathetically. Thank goodness, they had arrived at the Coppers' back door. Smokey pulled the emergency brake, jumped out, and ran around the car to open the car doors for them.

"You take care now, and be back by nine-thirty!" called Mrs. Copper from the house, and exchanged grins with Smokey before he made a wide U-turn and went roaring back out the driveway.

Making jam didn't turn out to be so difficult after all. Mrs. Copper had already washed the berries and picked out all the bugs, so as soon as they had washed and scalded the jars and set them upside down to drain, all that had to be done was to cook the berries, sugar, and lemon juice in a big kettle for a few minutes, and then skim it and ladle it into the jars. Mrs. Copper let Mama do most of it and kept telling her how well she did it—just like a born cook, she said.

Then Mrs. Copper poured a little melted paraffin into each jar and left them to cool. There were a few pots to wash, and that was the end of it.

"So, now you know how to make raspberry jam," said Mrs. Copper, smiling.

Mama's eyes were bright. "Why, there was nothing to it! It's a lot easier than making bread."

"You caught right on to that, too," said Mrs. Copper, who had taught Mama that skill right after Papa left.

"Yes," replied Mama. "It costs less, and Julia Jarvis told me to use part whole-wheat flour so it's extra good for the children."

"Is that right? I'll have to try that," said Mrs. Copper.

"Can we play with Jack?" asked Martin, who didn't

like sitting still for long. For once, Mrs. Copper let the friendly dog into the house, where even Sarah enjoyed patting him and rolling a ball to him.

A little later, Mr. Copper came in from his chores and brought out his arrowhead collection for the children to see, explaining where he had found each one—mostly while plowing fields. He was not as talkative as his wife, but had a kind twinkle in his eye, and they liked him. Before they knew it, they heard the car pull in—Smokey was back.

"You made it back right at nine-thirty, Smokey," said Aunt Hazel. "I was afraid you might meet up with some pretty girls and forget the time."

Smokey shook his head solemnly.

"You know I wouldn't do that, Aunt Hazel. I always do just what you tell me."

The two of them chuckled, sharing a private joke.

Franny tried not to pay any attention, but she found that her teeth were tightly clenched. Why should Smokey Manning get to call her "Aunt Hazel" in that familiar voice?

She's my friend, too. I wish I could call her "Aunt Hazel," she thought. But she wasn't sure what Mrs. Copper would think about that.

The evening had left Franny with a warm feeling, and she was thankful that Smokey did not have much to say on the ride home. Their little family had been special guests of the Coppers, and it would be too bad if Smokey Manning spoiled that, too.

CHAPTER 12

Breakthrough

Gil came to the door the next morning at the usual time, but Franny immediately noticed something different about him. His gray eyes were sparkling with excitement, and he couldn't stop smiling. There was no sign of the stubborn mask he had worn when she first saw him at school.

Mama paused from the bread she was kneading, noticing it, too.

"Gil—you are looking so handsome—er—so happy today!"

Franny was surprised to hear Mama say something like that and was even more surprised when Gil forgot to blush.

"Look," he said, pulling a thin, coverless book out of

his pocket. He held it up, opened it randomly, and placed his fingers carefully on the page. Franny and Mama stared at him dumbly.

"Listen to this!" Gil cleared his throat and began reading. "From - his - lookout - at - the - top - of - the - canyon - wall—" His voice faltered, then continued with determination. "Jed-could-see-the-three-horsemen-on - the - trail - below. The on—*one*—riding - the - black - stallion - had - to - be - the - leader - of - the - gang - who - had - held - up—"

Mama and Franny looked at each other in amazement. Gil was *reading*. It was not smooth or fluent—the words came out in choppy little bunches—but he was getting nearly every word, reading a page of print better than he had ever done before.

"How did you do that?" asked Franny suspiciously.

"It's wonderful!" gasped Mama.

"You're fooling us," guessed Franny. "I'll bet you memorized it from a radio program."

In answer, Gil thrust the book at her, his finger pointing to the passage he had just read.

"Well, then, why can you read this book when you can't read any of the others?"

"I guess Smokey taught me."

"Smokey!"

"He brought over some of his books last night. He thought I might like them. Well, he tried to help me with them, but it was just like always—I just couldn't get the words right. So he started reading me this story. I mean, it's a really exciting story about this guy who—anyway, all kinds of things were happening, and just then Smokey said it was nine-thirty and he had to go. Well, I couldn't go to sleep without finding out how it ended. It's hard to explain—I just wanted to so much. I used markers like you showed me, Mrs. Parsons, and all of a sudden I was reading! I stayed up until two o'clock and finished the whole book!"

Mama had walked away from the bread dough, her hands still covered with flour. She studied Gil with amazement. "It's like a miracle. Does your mother know?"

Gil shook his head. "I could hardly hold it back," he said. "But just because I read one book—do you think I'll be able to read the schoolbooks now?"

Silently, Franny brought out the books they had been working with, laid them on the table, and opened one to a familiar page.

Gil sat down solemnly and adjusted the marker he had been using. Slowly and carefully, he proceeded from one line to the next, correcting himself over and over, but completing the page.

Mama forgot all about her floury hands and hugged Gil. She was laughing and crying at the same time.

"I'm so happy!" she exclaimed. "I always knew you'd be able to do it someday, but I never dreamed it would happen so soon. Oh, Gil!"

"All those things you taught me, Mrs. Parsons—they just seemed to come together and make sense last night.

And Franny—she's the one I have to thank most, because she started it all. Where did she go?"

It had all been too much for Franny. Instead of joy at hearing Gil read, she had felt a wrenching bitterness. Slipping quietly out the door, she ran for the refuge of the elderberry thicket, now jeweled with red, half-ripe clusters. She flung herself under a bush and beat the ground with her fists, clenching her jaws to hold back the full-blown screaming tantrum that wanted to erupt.

So Smokey Manning had done it again! It was his fault Papa had left and now he was taking credit for all the work she and Mama had done with Gil this summer. Standing up for Gil against people like the Websters had been hard, but she had done it because she thought it was right and important. But what had Smokey done? Coming in with his dime Western just when Gil was ready to read, and taking the credit. *God, did you make Smokey Manning just to torment me?*

She could not hold back the tears any longer—the anger, hurt, and loneliness she had been bottling up poured out to water the elderberry roots, while she tried to muffle her sobs in a clump of ryegrass. She heard Mama call, but she didn't answer and there was no second call.

Franny's outburst did not last long. She didn't like being a crybaby. "Always crying over spilled milk," Papa had said once. "That was your grandmother's style." Besides, deep inside she knew she was jealous, and that was not something Papa approved of, either.

· 100 ·

Why should she expect Gil to understand the pain she had gone through because of him? To Gil, she was just a spunky little girl who really hadn't been able to teach him much.

And could she blame him for seeing Smokey Manning as a hero? A good-looking friend five years older? How could he help being impressed? She even put aside the impulse to tell Gil about Smokey's brush with the law. What good would it do?

A long, shuddering sigh released the last of her anger, and she rose to her feet, wiping her tearstained face on her sleeve. She didn't feel like returning to the house just yet. Mama could listen to Gil read while she baked her bread, now that he was doing so much better. It would be a good time to hoe the potato patch.

Every time it rained, a new crop of quack grass sprang up between the rows, and Franny was soon whacking away. The thing about quack grass was that no matter how much you hoed it, it always popped up again. Just like Smokey Manning. Whack! Whack!

She didn't even pay attention when the rural mailman's familiar car crunched gravel from the curve by the bluff. Her hoe chopped out its steady rhythm as the car came closer. Unless there was a catalog or sale bill to deliver, the car seldom stopped. Today it paused for a second, then continued on toward Coppers'. Franny kept hoeing, but the nagging hope inside her would not leave. Another disappointment was not exactly what she needed right now, but she had to risk it.

RETA E. KING LIBRARY
CHADRON STATE COLLEGE
CHADRON, NE 69337

She laid down the hoe and marched briskly toward the mailbox. In one quick motion, she pulled down the door and reached for the contents.

The next minute, she was racing for the house, her heart pounding.

"Mama! Mama!" she screamed before she had even reached the door. "There's a letter from Papa!"

CHAPTER 13

Offerings

It was a thick envelope, with two stamps, and Mama's fingers trembled so much she could hardly tear it open. Page by page, she scanned the letter silently, while Gil, Franny, and Martin watched her face for clues to the message. Even Sarah seemed to realize that this was an anxious moment.

"What does he say? Where is he?" Franny was unable to wait for her mother to finish.

Mama was breathing fast and clasped the letter to her breast. "He says so much—I can't digest it all."

Gil, realizing that he was witnessing a private family matter, started toward the door with a hurried good-bye.

"Gil—tell Julia I'd like her to stop by. I need to talk to her about your reading, and—I may need some other advice, too. My husband has a job out West—I'm not sure what to do."

Gil nodded and left quietly.

"A job out West? What kind of job? Can we hear the letter?" Franny could not contain her excitement.

Mama sank into her favorite rocker and settled Sarah on her lap while the other children pressed close on each side as she read:

"My dearest Rosalyn, Franny, Martin, and Sarah:

I've been writing this letter for two months, but I promised myself I wouldn't send it until I had good news for you. As you'll see when you read it, I spent a lot of time chasing down false leads, and I got pretty depressed. But I've got a good job now, although I had to come a long way to get it. I ran into a fellow in Chicago who had just come back from the state of Washington. He'd been working on this big, new dam the government is building—the Grand Coulee, they call it—but he hurt his back and had to go home. He said they were hiring, if I could find a way out there. You'll read in another part of my letter what happened to the truck. Anyway, by that time I had no money left. So I snuck onto a freight train and "rode the rails" all the way up here. Believe me, that trip gave me adventures to entertain the little ones for a year! But I got here, and they hired me. It's hard labor and I'm mighty glad when I'm done at night, but the pay is good, and I'll be able to send money every month. This first money order is small, because

I had to buy some heavy boots and overalls, but they furnish barracks for us to live in, so you'll be able to pay rent to the Coppers and have money for your needs. Now I'll let you read the parts of the letter I wrote while I was still roaming around Chicago—and then we'll make some decisions."

Mama paused and her face was serious. "You see what it means—he won't be home for a long time."

"Read the rest, Mama," Martin said. "What else does he say?"

Mama shook her head. "It's too long. And Papa was very sad when he wrote it. Franny, you can read it if you like, and I'll put it away for when you're older, so you won't forget the hard times your father went through. . . ."

"What about the last page?" Franny asked. "What did he write on the last page?"

"That's the hard part," Mama said wearily. "But I'll read it to you." She flipped through the pages and found the last one, and read in a quiet voice:

"So now you know how bad things are, all over the country, and why I thank the Lord for sending me this job, even though it's fifteen hundred miles from my family. The worst part is that after it's finished—in 1940, they figure—it won't take more than a few people to keep it running, so there's no housing being built for families. This is an isolated part of the country. Spokane is the closest city, and that's one hundred *fifty miles away, with no roads to speak of up this way. That's why I think you'll be better off staying where you are, with folks you know and a roof over your heads. I asked about time off, and they said if things slow down in the winter, maybe I could get a couple of weeks off. That's not much to go on, I know, but I think I can face it, if you can. I'll have to know that you, Rosalyn, and the kids are strong enough to make your way all that time without me. I can send money, but I know a father's responsibility is much more than that. If you think I'm shirking it by working here, I'll come home in a minute. Now that I'm in one spot you can write to me often, so maybe I can help you with some problems from here. I know it will be a real joy to get letters from you and my little Franny. Teach Martin to write so he can send letters to Papa, too! I'll be waiting for the first letter, and please be honest, Rosalyn, in telling me how you feel about this. If it meant . . ."*

Mama folded the letter and stuffed it back in the envelope. "He just says a couple more things, and then good-bye," she murmured.

If it meant *what?* Franny could not even bear to think the words Mama had chosen not to read. She knew that sometimes when people are separated they stop loving each other, but such a thing had never seemed possible in this family. She shivered.

"I want Papa to come home." Tears of disappointment welled up in Martin's wide brown eyes.

"What do you think, Mama? Do you think we can get along for two **years?**" Franny asked.

· 106 ·

Mama stared at the envelope in her lap and stroked Sarah's hair absentmindedly. "I'm not sure," she whispered. Her eyes had a glazed, scared look, just like the day Papa had left.

"Mama!" Franny spoke sharply. "I want him home, too, but then it would be just like before he left. With no work, he'd feel bad all the time. I think we should let him stay. You've learned to do all the things he used to do for us."

"But two years, Franny—it's a long time. I never thought I'd be responsible for three children *all alone.*"

"You're not alone. The Coppers always help. And the people at church, Julia Jarvis and Gil—maybe even the Websters. And I promise to help. Why, in two years, I'll be fourteen."

"There's one other thing I could do," Mama said slowly.

"What's that?"

"I've thought about it some, but I kept hoping your papa would find a place for us. Now—well, I could ask your grandparents to take us in for a while."

"Our grandparents? We don't even know them!" Franny gasped at this news. "Where do they live?"

"Where I grew up, in a small town in southern Illinois. It doesn't get as cold there."

"But why haven't they ever come to see us? They don't even write to us."

"That's because—my mother—was angry at your papa. At both of us, really, because I ran away and married him when they didn't want me to."

"Why didn't she like Papa?" Martin asked. "Papa's a good man."

"But he grew up in an orphanage. He had no family, and they thought he was a drifter."

Franny did not like what she was hearing. "If they're so mad at you, I don't think they'd want all of *us.*"

"They just might, because Papa's not with us," Mama said softly. "They have a big house—"

"I don't want to live with someone who doesn't like Papa," said Franny. At last she understood why Papa always cautioned her not to act like her grand-mother.

"I want to ask Julia Jarvis what she thinks," Mama replied.

"What about Papa? You should write and ask him."

"Oh, I *know* what he'd think."

"If Papa doesn't want us to, we won't," Franny said flatly.

But she knew Mama was the grown-up. She would be the one to decide. Still, Franny didn't like the idea of being somebody's unwelcome guest and Mama needn't think she was going to cooperate.

It had been a topsy-turvy day of emotions, and although it wasn't even noon yet, Franny felt very tired. Much as she would have liked to share the news of Papa's job with Alice Faye, she didn't feel up to it.

"I think I'll go and tell Mrs. Copper about Papa's letter," she told her mother.

"All right, but don't say anything about—what I suggested."

"No, I won't," promised Franny as she started out the door. The nice thing about having so many friends was being able to choose just the right one to suit your mood. Right now, Franny needed Mrs. Copper.

Right after supper that night, Julia Jarvis bounced in the door, grinning from ear to ear. The first thing she did was to grab Mama and give her a big hug, and then she hugged Franny, Martin, and Sarah, too. They were all surprised, because Julia was usually so businesslike. But you couldn't blame her for being thrilled at Gil's progress.

"If it hadn't been for you, Franny, I wouldn't have had anyone to help Gil," she exclaimed. "And Rosalyn, you were the one with the insight to figure out what his problems were and how to solve them. I owe you both so much."

Mama shook her head modestly. Nobody had ever praised her much. "Gil's the one who deserves credit," she said. "He came here every day for more than six weeks and kept trying so hard. He really did it himself. And of course, Smokey Manning helped, too."

"All *he* did was give Gil that book." Franny didn't miss the chance to give her opinion, but Julia stood looking at her with wise gray eyes, so much like her son's, and smiled gently.

"No, Franny. Smokey Manning gave Gil much more

than the book. Much more. You may not understand it right now, but someday you will. I'm grateful to Smokey Manning, too. But"—she turned to Mama—"I understand that you have some good news, too. Tell me about it."

Mama got out Papa's letter and read parts of it, filling in details in her own words.

Julia looked thoughtful. "Two years. Well, I guess that's a reasonable price to pay for a good job in these times."

Mama shot her a peeved glance, as though she had expected more sympathy than that. "I don't think I can stand it," she said.

Julia took Mama's hand. "Of course you can, Rosalyn. Just look how well you've done these first few months. You've learned to do so much for yourself. Why, by the time your husband comes back, you won't need him at all."

"I'll *always* need James!" cried Mama, trying to pull back her hand. "How can you say a thing like that?"

Julia held on firmly. "Of course you'll *want* him back. That's the way it should be, and it's different from *needing* him. You're learning to be self-reliant."

Mama was not pleased at all and managed to jerk her hand away.

"You're talking about yourself, Julia—not me. I'll never be self-reliant. I'm thinking of writing my parents and asking them to take us in."

"Your parents?" Julia's eyebrows shot up. "Didn't you

tell me once that they had disowned—" She stopped short, glancing at the children. "I mean, are you sure that would be wise?"

"They can't do more than say no," said Mama. "I thought of it before, but as long as there was a chance we could join James, I held on here. But honestly, Julia— the truth is—I haven't seen them for over ten years. I miss them."

"It's sad," agreed Julia. "A rift in families is always sad. You'd like your children to know their grandparents—family ties are important. Yes, I think you should try to make peace with them. But not by begging them to take you in. Don't you see how that will make your husband look in their eyes? When you go back to them, Rosalyn, you need to go back strong, not weak. Do you understand what I'm saying?"

Mama nodded slightly, but looked unhappy.

"Besides," Julia's voice became cheerful again, "you have your work cut out for you the rest of the summer, Miz Parsons. I'm going to preregister Gil at the Longfield High School tomorrow, and I intend to ask the principal for some materials to prepare Gil for his classes. I'm sure he'll need to study hard the rest of the summer, and you've proved yourself to be the best tutor in this part of the country. You can't desert your star pupil!"

"Just for the summer, I suppose. . . ." Mama started to give in, and Julia was quick to take advantage.

"Good. It's settled then. Don't make any hasty decisions until the summer is over."

CHAPTER 14

Moving Wheels

It was another sky blue day, with the ripe smell of mid-August in the air. The garden had outdone itself—Mama and Mrs. Copper had spent the last few weeks canning beans, and now worked on the endless tomatoes.

With Mama down at Mrs. Copper's house, Franny and Gil had cut short the lessons and were outside on the grass playing with the little ones.

Franny smiled as she watched Gil crouch on all fours, his long legs at odd angles, delighting Martin and Sarah.

"Cr-*aaa-aaak. Cr-aaa-aaak.* The big chicken's gonna get you, Sarah!" he teased.

"I wish Darlene could see you now," Franny said, laughing.

Gil blushed. "Darlene? Who's Darlene?"

"Don't try to pretend you don't know. I heard you met a girl at a dance who thinks you're cute. First thing you know, you'll be as bad as Smokey Manning."

She knew that was the best compliment she could pay him, because he went everywhere with Smokey these days—ball games, country dances, sometimes just fishing. And it was true, more than once she had heard about their giving rides home to some of the local girls.

After his chicken act had been exhausted, Gil moved to a sitting position under the tree. He reached into his pocket, pulled out a comb, and swept the tousled hair back from his forehead.

"Oh, no!" groaned Franny. "You're even starting to *act* like him."

"Like who?" asked Gil innocently.

"You know who. Of all the people in the world, I don't know why you'd want to copy *him.*"

"I wish you wouldn't hate Smokey so much, Franny," said Gil, suddenly serious. "He's just like a brother to me."

Franny squirmed. "I guess you wouldn't like him so much if he'd come and taken *your* papa's job away from him. Papa would still be here with us if it wasn't for Smokey Manning."

"Do you hear from your pa often?"

"Yes, he writes every week now. And I've sent him three letters already. It sure is good to be able to write to him about stuff."

"What stuff?"

"Stuff I worry about. Except I'm not supposed to tell him about Mama taking us away to live with her parents."

"She's not gonna do that, is she?" Gil looked alarmed.

Franny shrugged. "I don't know. She doesn't say anything, but I think she'll decide before school starts."

"Tell her I'll help her with chores. I don't think you should move away, and neither does my mom."

"I'd like to have a grandma," Martin piped up. "Grandmas make good cookies."

"Who told you that?" Franny pushed at Martin playfully. "You've got Mrs. Copper to make cookies for you. You don't want to go away, do you?"

"I've got to go," said Gil, checking his watch. "I have to mow the minister's lawn. Then after lunch, he'll drive me over to Longfield. Today's my entrance exam."

"Wait, we'll walk partway with you," said Franny, scrambling to her feet. "I've been promising Alice Faye all summer that I'd bring Martin and Sarah over, and I haven't done it yet."

They each took one of Sarah's little hands, and she toddled on between them happily, with Martin skipping on ahead.

"I hear Smokey is making elderberry wine," said Franny as they passed through the thicket, which a few weeks before had hung black with berries.

"Uh-huh. He's got a secret recipe. It belonged to his aunt Hazel's father."

"Oh, boy. She trusted *him* with a secret recipe? Well, I hope it's better than elderberry pie. Ugh! I was glad when Mama gave the berries away."

By this time Sarah was tired of walking, and Gil swung her high on his shoulder. She squealed with joy and hugged his neck.

When they reached the Webster house, Alice Faye was not in sight, but her mother was out in front tending her flower garden. She wore a large-brimmed white hat and long gloves to protect her arms from the sun.

"We certainly could use some rain," she remarked in her sweet, proper voice. "I just had to come out and give these poor flowers a little drinky. I'm sorry to say that Alice Faye isn't home right now. She went to the library with her brother, Charles. She'll be disappointed, I'm sure."

"Yes," Franny said. "She always asks me to bring my little brother and sister over—she really loves them. It's hard to bring them, though—especially Sarah. She always wants to be carried. I wish Alice Faye could come to *our* house more often."

"Well—uh—" Mrs. Webster got very busy plucking a dried-up blossom. Then she looked up at Gil, with a puzzled expression. "Franny, I don't believe I've met your friend. Would you please introduce me?"

Franny held her breath, wondering if Gil could handle the situation. "I'm sorry, Mrs. Webster. I thought you knew him. This is Gil Jarvis."

Mrs. Webster's eyes popped open wide, and before

she could speak, Gil, still holding Sarah, took a step toward her, offering an outstretched hand. "Pleased to meet you, Mrs. Webster," he said, remembering to smile.

Mrs. Webster seemed stunned as she weakly returned the handshake. "Julia Jarvis's son? My goodness, I just didn't recognize you. You look—uh—taller." She gave an uncertain little laugh. "That's the way with children—if we don't see you for a few months, you grow up on us!"

"Gil is on his way to lunch at the minister's house," said Franny, enjoying Mrs. Webster's confusion. "So I guess if Alice Faye's not home, I'll have to take Martin and Sarah back home again. It was nice seeing you, Mrs. Webster."

"Yes, indeed. I'll tell her you were here. And Gil—it has been a real pleasure meeting you. I hope to see you again."

Franny lifted Sarah from Gil's arms and, together with Martin, started home. By the time she had reached the thicket, she was laughing out loud. If anyone needed proof of Gil's coming out of his shell, this was it. He had managed to impress Mrs. Webster!

The three children stopped at home for their favorite lunch of tomato sandwiches—thick, golden brown slices of Mama's whole-wheat bread, soaked deep red and juicy with ripe tomatoes. When they finished, they went on their way again, down to the Copper farm, where

Mama was canning. They played quietly on the big front porch, where Mama could keep an eye on them, but away from kitchen dangers, such as scalding water and hot jars. Franny laid Sarah's quilt on the shabby porch couch, where the little girl soon cuddled up for a nap. Martin insisted on playing checkers, but Franny soon lost patience with his made-up "rules" and turned to the pile of old books that Mrs. Copper had brought out for them.

She had become quite interested in *Rebecca of Sunnybrook Farm* when she heard the sound of a truck and looked up to see a Webster Lumber Company delivery truck rumbling into the yard. It crossed the farmyard and went up the little hillside to where the old granary had been.

Since the fire (the very day Papa had left, Franny remembered sadly), Mr. Copper and Smokey had torn down the damaged remains, but now intended to build a new granary on the old foundation. Both men left their work and hurried across the yard to meet the lumber truck.

"There's Smokey!" chirped Martin. "I'm going to talk to him. All right, Franny?"

"I s'pose. Don't get in the way, though."

"Where do you want this stuff piled?" yelled the truck driver.

Franny watched him jump out of the truck and walk over to talk to Mr. Copper and Smokey. Smokey took time to tousle Martin's brown hair, and then the three men moved off in the direction of the old granary, pointing and talking.

Franny looked down at her book, but glanced up again to the hillside. There stood Martin, behind the lumber truck, his hands in his overalls pockets, trying to copy Smokey's stance. What a little monkey!

Smiling, she returned to her book. She was still searching for the sentence where she had left off when an unexplainable feeling caused her to look again toward Martin. For a second it seemed that nothing had changed, but then she saw it—the wheels of the driverless truck were moving—the heavy lumber truck was rolling slowly backward in the direction of her little brother!

Panic seized her and she fought off its freezing grip. "Martin!!" The jagged scream tore her throat. She leaped forward and ran wildly, knowing that she could never cross the yard in time to save him.

On the hillside, Smokey whirled around at the sound of the scream and saw what was happening. In one frantic motion, he raced toward Martin, thrusting him violently out of the truck's backward path just as it bore down on him. The overhanging lumber struck Smokey's shoulder, knocking him off his feet and under the faster-turning wheels rolling down the hill.

The next instant, everyone was yelling. Martin lay shrieking in the dirt, and as the truck rolled to a stop near the driveway, Franny's horrified eyes saw Smokey crumpled on the ground, one leg twisted like an injured grasshopper. She ran to Martin and hugged him, burying her face against his shirt, trying to shut out the reality of what had happened. As the men bent over Smokey, Mama and Mrs. Copper came running across the yard, their faces frightened.

"He's all right, Mama—Martin's all right. . . ."

As Mama tearfully took her little boy into her arms, Franny, her whole body shivering, forced herself to look again at Smokey Manning. His aunt Hazel's huge body was crouched on the ground next to him, her face white as the dishtowel she still clutched in her hand.

"Oh, my boy, my poor boy," she moaned, one rough hand feeling for the pulse. His mouth hung open and his skin had a bluish cast.

"We've got to get him to a doctor, quick," said Mr. Copper, his voice quivering. "Let me help you, Hazel. He's breathing, ain't he?"

"Looks like a bash on his head," said the truck driver, also badly shaken. "Them boards hit him head-on."

"He's breathin', but shallow," said Mrs. Copper huskily. "Oh, my poor, poor baby."

"That left leg looks pretty bad," added her husband. "George, find a board to put under it before we move him. I'm going to get the car."

While Carl Copper brought the car around, his wife was still on the ground beside the injured Smokey, gently massaging his wrists and chest, carefully stroking his face. And it was Hazel Copper whose strong arms

· 119 ·

eased Smokey onto the board. As she lifted the injured leg, he moaned weakly and his eyelids fluttered.

"There, there, son, you'll be all right. Aunt Hazel's takin' care of you," she crooned.

There was barely room for the outstretched legs and board in the car, but Mrs. Copper managed to squeeze in, still supporting his head and shoulders.

"Call the hospital and tell them we're comin'," she said as Mr. Copper put the car in gear and started forward.

Martin's crying finally subsided and Mama carried him toward the house. "Is Smokey going to be all right, Mama?" he asked, between sniffles.

"I hope so, Martin," Mama said fervently. "He saved your life."

Sarah was still asleep on the porch, and the kitchen was in a disarray of half-filled jars and simmering kettles.

Mama stared at the telephone. "It's been so long since I used one—" she murmured. She laid Martin on the couch and then firmly cranked the phone. "Operator? Give me the Longfield Hospital."

It was late afternoon by the time Mama had finished canning the batch of tomatoes and cleaned the kitchen. She walked with Franny and the little ones back up the dusty road. They were all quiet—still shocked by the afternoon's tragedy. Franny usually admired the beautiful bowers of goldenrod, blue chicory and Queen Anne's lace that lined the ditches and hedgerows, but now she scarcely noticed them.

Her feelings were in a turmoil. She relived again and again that awful moment when she had seen the truck start to roll toward Martin. She felt a need to touch him—to make sure that solid little body was really safe. But then there was another feeling—the sickness she had felt at the sight of Smokey Manning's crumpled body. Instinctively, she had prayed that he was not dead. It had been easy, being hateful to him even when he tried to be nice. It seemed there would always be time to change her mind. Only now there might be no time. *Please God, give me a chance to make it up to him.*

Later, around the dinner table, Mama bowed her head, something she had not done since Papa left.

"Let's all offer a prayer tonight," she said. "Lord, you have blessed us in many ways. Even when things were darkest, you watched over us. You've given us friends, you've given James a new job, and today you spared our little Martin. Please God, I want to ask one more thing— let Smokey Manning be all right."

"Please, God," echoed Martin.

"Please, God." Franny's prayer was only a whisper.

"And dear Lord," Mama continued, "please help me find a way to protect these children until we can all be together again. Amen."

They were clearing the table when they heard a car pull up.

Mama caught her breath. "Maybe it's the Coppers," she said.

"No, it's a lady." Martin had run to the window to see.

A gray-haired lady in a seersucker dress was coming to the door. Mama welcomed her in.

"I'm Miss Spinney, a teacher supervisor from the county school superintendent's office," she explained. "I've just tested Gil Jarvis. Can I talk to you about him for a few minutes?"

"Oh, my—" Mama glanced at the crude furnishings of the kitchen, which was their everyday living space. "Would you like to come in the parlor?"

Franny held her breath. The only furnishings in the parlor were the heating stove, an old easy chair that Papa had never gotten around to repairing, and some boxes full of Papa's books.

The lady shook her head. "This is fine," she said, and smiled, choosing Mama's rocker. "Mrs. Parsons, I'm amazed at the change in Gil this summer. I've known about his reading problems for years. His mother has begged for help and I've suggested methods to his teachers, but I'm afraid they haven't been effective. We've heard of some new theories being advanced out East, but there's no material available here yet. Now, by some miracle, he studies with you for a couple of months and makes unbelievable progress. How did you accomplish this?"

Mama opened her hands simply. "*Gil* is the one who accomplished it. He just came here at the right time. He wanted so strongly to go to high school. My daughter

Franny helped him get started and gradually we both helped him with other things."

"*What* other things?" The lady eyed Mama sharply. "Mrs. Jarvis tells me you thought he was seeing words backward, or something like that."

"Oh, yes. When you hear someone read every day, you can't help but learn from the kinds of mistakes they make. Then we showed him how to correct those mistakes. There were a lot of ways of doing that, and Gil caught right on to them. He's a very smart boy, you know."

"It seems that until now, Mrs. Jarvis was the only one who believed that," the supervisor said drily. "But Mrs. Parsons, if you only knew *how many* children are going through school branded as 'dummies' because of reading problems. I'll bet there are as many as ten parents just in the Longfield area who would pay you wages to tutor their children, if you could do for them what you did for Gil. Not only that, but my office would like to hire you part-time to advise our teachers about your methods."

"Oh, no, no, no. I couldn't. I'm not a teacher!" Mama's eyes were glazing and her hands twisted together. That was a sure sign she was upset. "I didn't even go to college. I was all ready to go, but then I got married instead. Now I have my family to take care of."

"I understand that. But couldn't you still—"

Trembling, Mama reached for the door and held it open. "I don't like to be rude, but you're asking too much. We're waiting for word about a dear friend who was badly injured. . . . I just can't talk about these things anymore."

"I'm sorry." The lady rose quickly to leave. "It was bad timing, I'm sure. But I'll be in touch again."

When she had gone, Mama leaned against the door, her eyes closed and her breath coming in uneven gusts.

"Are you going to cry, Mama?" Martin asked anxiously.

Mama opened her eyes and forced a smile. "No. No, Martin, I'm fine. Just tired, that's all. Let's get these dishes out of the way and then you little ones can be off to bed. I need to rest—and do some thinking."

After the younger children had been tucked into bed, Franny sat with a book under the white flicker of the Aladdin lamp, watching her mother out of the corner of her eye. After a while, Mama brought out her pen and letter paper.

"Are you going to write to Papa?" asked Franny.

"No—not tonight." She paused a minute, then went on slowly, "I think it's time to write to my mother and father."

Across the big table, Mama wrote her letter—a few words at a time, pausing often to nibble the end of her pen. At nine o'clock, when Franny went to bed, she was still not finished.

Tired as she was, it was not easy for Franny to get to sleep. Scenes of the accident replayed themselves over and over in her mind. Martin standing with his hands in his pockets, just like Smokey, with the truck rolling back toward him—her scream—Smokey's sudden dash—then Smokey lying limp and broken on the ground—the pain in Mrs. Copper's face as she knelt beside him. Then she thought of Gil, who probably didn't even know yet. Without Smokey, what would become of Gil? At last she dozed off, but her dreams were full of the same grim images.

CHAPTER 15

Pulling Together

Franny woke early the next morning, just when the birds back in the elderberry thicket were making their own wake-up racket. She heard Mama in the kitchen, building the fire, and Sarah jabbering softly to herself in her crib. It seemed like Martin was the only one who could sleep—not bothered at all that he had almost been killed the day before. Maybe he didn't even understand how close he had come.

She was tempted to slip back to sleep for a while, but decided to get up and get dressed after all. It seemed important to stick close to Mama for a few days. After such a scare, it was hard to tell what she might do.

Mama gave Franny a wan smile, but her eyes looked

like she hadn't slept much. Franny glanced over at the windowsill where the mail was kept. There was the letter, neatly addressed, sealed, and stamped.

Mama saw her staring at it. "It's not definite," she said. "They may not even answer."

So she *had* asked them. "Papa likes to think of us being here, in the house he fixed for us!" Franny's blue eyes begged her mother to understand.

"I know, Franny—but I just wish it were safer. Every time the wind blows, I'm afraid!"

"Well, *I'm* not," Franny said stubbornly. "Papa said it was built sturdily. That's why it lasted so long, even when nobody lived in it."

"I'm making some cocoa. It'll be ready in a minute." Sure, it was just like Mama to avoid an argument by changing the subject. She had been doing it a lot lately.

"After breakfast," she continued, "I think we should walk down to see Hazel."

"All of us? I could stay with Sarah and—"

"I think we should all go," Mama said quietly. "There should be some news by now."

It was eight o'clock by the time the four of them walked down the road to the Copper farm. Mr. Copper was doing morning chores, and Mrs. Copper invited them into her big kitchen. The rows of canned tomatoes still stood where Mama had left them yesterday, along with an assortment of bowls and covered pans.

"Some of the people from town brung in food," Mrs.

Copper explained. "They want to help, but they don't know how. You folks take some of it on home. I don't know what to do with it."

Mrs. Copper found chairs for them and sank down into her own sturdy chair beside the table. Had her hair always been so gray? For some reason, it seemed to Franny that she looked ten years older than usual.

"How is he?" asked Mama.

Mrs. Copper nodded. "He's gonna be all right. Concussion—leg broken—lots of bruises—nothing that won't heal." She seemed ready to cry.

"That's very good news," said Mama, with relief in her voice. "Young folks can mend fast. But you look so sad, Hazel. Is something else wrong?"

Mrs. Copper let out a deep, quivering sigh. "It should be good news. It *would* be, if we hadn't made the mistake of calling his mother. I wish we hadn't—when he came to, he was askin' for me an' Carl, and askin' about little Marty—never mentioned his ma, but we thought it was the right thing to do, so we called her."

"And?"

"She got somebody to bring her—got up to the hospital about eight o'clock last night. They had given Smokey some anesthetic while they set his leg, and he was feeling kind of low about then—started blaming himself for the whole thing. Can you beat that? He thought it was his fault Marty came out by that truck. He was sayin' he was nothin' but trouble to us and all that kind of stuff. Well, we was tellin' him it wasn't true, you know, but then about that time his ma pranced in, and oh, dear God . . ." Mrs. Copper put her face in her hands and sniffled.

Mama reached out timidly and patted her shoulder. "There—it'll be all right," she said, just like when one of her kids came crying with a stubbed toe.

Mrs. Copper cleared her throat. "Oh, she put on a great scene! This was what we'd done to her little boy. She ranted and raved—said she had a call in to the judge to get his probation shortened. As soon as he can be moved, she's taking him home."

Franny's heart leaped. "Then Papa can come back!" she cried.

The second the words were out, she knew she had made a terrible mistake. It was as though she had struck Mrs. Copper across the face.

"Franny!" Mama looked shocked and angry. "Can't you see this is no time for—"

Mrs. Copper put her head down again. "I guess I know now how you folks felt. Remember how I had no time for Smokey when he first came here? He didn't know beans from barley, but by golly, he wouldn't give up on anything. I had to admire his spunk—and then little by little, we just started thinkin' of him as our boy. And I think he felt the same about us. But now, this. Yes, Franny, I s'pose you can let your dad know. We'd be glad to have him back."

"I'm sorry. I didn't mean—" Franny forced the words out. For the first time, she began to understand how hard it must be for grown-ups. Like even if you're happy, you *can't* be happy when somebody else is sad. No wonder Mama had such a hard time!

Mrs. Copper's big hand reached out across the table and grabbed Franny's tough little callused one. "It's all right, honey. We all got our crosses to bear."

"At least it's a relief that Smokey's not critically injured," said Mama. "I'll be grateful to him forever for saving Martin."

Mr. Copper came in then, along with one of the many neighbors who had offered to help with his work. After a few words with him, Mama made an excuse to leave. They had left a note for Gil, and he would be waiting when they got back.

He was. In fact, he was pacing back and forth on the grass by their house, and when he caught sight of them, he came to meet them.

Sarah reached out her arms to him, and Mama was glad to hand her over—she was getting heavy to carry.

"How is he?" were Gil's first anxious words.

Mama managed a cheerful smile. "He's going to be fine, Gil. Nothing that won't heal. He has a concussion and broken leg. And a lot of bruises, I'm sure. He did a brave thing."

"People were talking about it downtown. That was the first I heard. Are you okay, Martin?"

Martin danced around to show him that he was. Franny wondered if her mother would say anything about Smokey leaving, but nothing was said. She decided to keep her own mouth shut this time. One blunder was enough for the day.

"You know I took a test yesterday," Gil said shyly as he got his books ready for studying. "At the high school. The teacher who gave it said I was doing well. She thinks I'll be able to catch up if I work real hard."

"I know. She came to see me last night." Mama pressed her lips together and looked at the floor. Perhaps she was thinking that she had made a blunder, too. "I—I sent her off in a kind of hurry. I hope she doesn't think I was rude. But I was tired, and upset about Smokey. What she said is really true, Gil. You are bright enough to overcome all those problems."

Franny couldn't resist a jibe. "Don't tell him that, Mama, or he'll never talk to plain people like us anymore."

Gil gave her a good-natured punch on the shoulder. "Sure, you 'plain people.' I get the idea that teacher thinks you're kind of special, too. Both of you. She told me there are a lot of people like me and she wishes there were more people with a gift for helping like you did."

Then Gil sat down to study. His work was harder these days, and it was all Franny could do to keep up with him. She was learning far above her own grade level. But it was exciting. She had always loved books, and now she found a real thirst for knowledge. One way or another, she would go to college someday.

An hour later, when they took a break from studying, Franny was surprised to notice that her mother, who usually kept very busy with housework in the morning, was standing by the kitchen window, staring out in a reverie. When she realized that Franny was watching her, she quickly began dusting windowsills, but later, when they were studying, Franny again noticed her standing lost in thought.

"Do you suppose Smokey can have visitors?" Gil asked, as he was getting ready to leave. "My mom is doing calls in our neighborhood this afternoon, and I'll bet she'd let me take the car, if you think it would be all right. I sure want to see him."

"I think you're supposed to be sixteen," Mama said. "But you're tall—who's going to know?" She grabbed the back of a chair and wrinkled her forehead as though a sudden thought had struck her.

"Gil—take me with you. I want to see him, too." At Gil's look of surprise, she added lamely, "I do want to tell him how grateful I am."

They were interrupted by a call from outside. "Yoo-hoo!" Alice Faye came skipping down the path from the elderberry thicket, her blond curls bobbing. She was pulling a big red wagon.

Franny ran to meet her. "Yoo-hoo!" she called, although Alice Faye could see her plainly. The old signal made her smile. Not long ago, they had been carefree little girls. Somehow, Franny felt that that was no longer true. The hard work this summer without Papa, Gil's progress, and especially the mixed feelings she had been having since the accident—it was all making her grow up faster than she would have thought possible.

Alice Faye pointed proudly at the wagon. "It's for Martin and Sarah," she said. "I never play with it anymore, and Mama said it would come in handy for pulling the little ones so's you don't always have to carry them—Sarah, anyway. You can have it for keeps."

"Oh, Alice Faye! It's so beautiful—thank you—come and show it to Mama!" She had never thought Mrs. Webster would do something so generous.

It seemed like Mama hadn't either, because for no reason at all, she just started crying.

CHAPTER 16

August Harvest

Alice Faye would have stayed all day, having the time of her life playing "mother" to Martin and Sarah, pulling them around in the red wagon, but Charles came looking for her.

"Did you forget that Mother told you to be home by lunchtime?" he asked. "Franny, isn't my sister the most forgetful person you ever met?"

In spite of his complaints, Charles seemed friendly and took a few minutes to help Franny pump a pail of fresh water to take to the house. The news of Papa's job had already spread through Fisher's Glen, and Charles said he was glad. Then he paused and changed the subject.

"I've been hearing some things about Gil Jarvis," he

said carefully. "I guess he's changed a lot. Even my mother says so."

"When you get to know him, he's really nice," said Franny. "He's going to high school this fall, you know."

"That so? Well, I hope he gets along all right."

Franny knew Charles too well to expect an apology or even an admission of being wrong, but she was happy that they were friends again.

After Charles and Alice Faye had left, Mama served lunch and then put Martin and Sarah in for naps.

"After what happened yesterday, I'm afraid to let you children out of my sight," Mama said nervously. "But I do want to go with Gil to the hospital. When they wake up, if I'm not back yet, take them over to Hazel's. It will be easy, now that we have the Websters' wagon, and I won't worry, knowing you're with the Coppers."

"Won't the Coppers be going back to the hospital?" Franny asked.

"Not until after chores this evening, I'm sure," said Mama. "I'll have Gil drop me off there when we get back."

Mama changed into her blue Sunday dress without even asking Franny whether it was right for the occasion, and a few minutes later Gil arrived and they drove off together.

The house suddenly seemed very quiet. Franny sat in her mother's rocker, pushing it back and forth gently with a toe that had found its way out the end of her badly worn shoes. She surveyed the room lovingly, not seeing cracked plaster and primitive furnishings, but a home that love had built. A home that she did not want to leave—at least not until Papa came for them.

She looked at the windowsill. The letter to her grandparents was still there. She wondered why her mother hadn't taken it out before the mailman went. *Let your dad know . . . we'd be glad to have him back,* Mrs. Copper had said. Maybe that was why Mama was so anxious to see Smokey—to make sure he was really going.

Franny stopped rocking. She felt uncomfortable, as though she had eaten too much lunch, even though she had only nibbled half a tomato sandwich. She got up and moved about the room. She found herself staring at the wooden rectangle that served as a latch on the closet door back in the corner. She forced the latch to its vertical position and opened the door.

Stale, hot air poured out of the closet, but she pushed aside the hanging coats and reached back in the corner until her fingers found the neck of Papa's old guitar.

She took it out carefully and touched its scuffed body, the worn strings hanging loose now, and thought about how Papa had looked when he used to play—all of them laughing and singing. It seemed so long since she had circled that happy day on the calendar.

She held the guitar in front of her and tightened the strings, trying to tune it like Papa had. The pegs slipped and the only sounds she could make were tinny whines. No one but Papa could make music on this guitar.

"If he comes back, everything will be like it used to be," she whispered.

But she knew it wasn't true. Things would always be different because Smokey had been here. Gil would be lonely again. Hazel Copper would grieve for the boy she had taken to her heart. There would be no job for Smokey, and he would probably fall in with his old companions back on the street corners of Milwaukee.

She replaced the guitar in the closet, closing the door on the past. As for the future, that was too confusing to think about.

After a while, she heard Sarah stirring and went to get the children up from their naps. They woke up noisy and boisterous, and for once she was glad.

"Wash your face, Martin, and put on your shoes. Mama wants us to go over to Coppers' until she gets back."

"Will you pull us in the wagon?"

"I sure will. It will be nice not having to carry fat Sarah anymore," Franny teased, hugging her baby sister. "Let me wash your face, Sarah. We're going bye-bye."

"Bye-bye, bye-bye," cooed the little girl, waving.

A few minutes later, they were on the way down the road. The wagon's rubber wheels rolled easily along the grassy shoulder. Martin sat behind, with little Sarah up front, between his knees.

"Look, there's a car in the Coppers' yard," Franny said, as they came near the farm. "I hope they won't mind our coming while they have company."

She turned the wagon into the driveway and noticed that the car was not a familiar one. A man was sitting behind the wheel, as though waiting for someone.

Loud voices were coming from the house—or, as she decided when they got closer, *one* very loud voice. It was a woman and she sounded angry.

"A shameful situation—" "Just what I should expect—" Franny could hear bits and pieces, but unsure what to do, she pulled the wagon up the sidewalk leading to the front veranda.

"Wait here," she whispered to Martin, and tiptoed closer to the screen door.

Franny could see the profile of the woman who was yelling. She was very thin and was dressed like a young woman. Her short, blue-black hair jutted in a stylish curve across her rouged cheek, but anger pushed out the veins in her face, giving away her age. Franny realized that she must be Smokey's mother.

"I should have known better, I see that now." Her shrill voice hurt Franny's ears. "I know you've always hated me, Hazel, and you saw your chance to get back at me. You taught my son all your crude, farmer ways. I asked for help and this is the thanks I get—my boy lying crippled and still wanting to stay with you. I saw his hands, Hazel—the palms covered with calluses. You've been getting slave labor from my Smokey all summer, while what he needed was fresh air and getting away from the pressures—"

Smokey's mother stopped for breath, sobbing and dabbing at her eyes. Surely now Mrs. Copper would tell her a thing or two. But Mrs. Copper was sitting silently on the sofa, her face blocked from Franny's view by a table lamp.

Her silence seemed to infuriate Smokey's mother, who started in even more angrily. "You may not know this, Hazel, but I warned my brother forty years ago not to marry you. He could have done so much better. Obviously, the only reason he married a bumpkin like you was for your farm. Well, you grabbed my brother, Hazel, and now you're trying to grab my son. But you're not going to get away with it. There's going to be a lawsuit about this."

"It's nobody's fault, Lena—" Mrs. Copper's voice was low and husky.

"It *is* your fault," screamed Smokey's mother, lurching across the room toward her sister-in-law. "And you're going to pay for it dearly!"

"Oh!" Mrs. Copper gasped, as the sound of a slap reached Franny's ears.

It reminded her of the day Tony had beaten Gil. Well, this time she was not going to stand by and do nothing. She burst into the room.

"Stop it right now!" she screamed.

Both women turned and looked at her. Except for a red mark on one cheek, Mrs. Copper's face was pale and perspiring and she was shivering.

Franny ran to her and threw her arms around her.

"Are you all right, Aunt Hazel?" she asked anxiously. Mrs. Copper nodded, but she didn't look all right.

Franny turned to Lena Manning.

"You'd better go," she said. "Go back to Milwaukee and leave Smokey alone. He doesn't need someone like you."

"This is none of your business, girl," Lena snapped. "I've come to take my son home where he can get the care he needs. A mother knows what's best for her son."

"Aunt Hazel, can I get you a glass of water?" Franny was worried at the way Mrs. Copper was acting.

"Y-yes. And my pills. There on the cupboard."

"She's sick, can't you see?" Franny turned her back on Lena and attended to Mrs. Copper, helping her to lie back on the couch.

Lena continued to pace and sniff, but showed no signs of leaving.

"Ma'am," said Franny, "I'd appreciate it if you'd look out the door and see if my little brother and sister are all right."

"I'm not here to play nursemaid—"

Shaking her head, Franny watched Mrs. Copper wash down her pills, and then went to the door herself.

"Martin, please bring Sarah in here."

Carefully, the little boy guided Sarah up the steps and through the doorway. He went to Mrs. Copper and hugged her. Then he looked at Lena with his wide brown eyes. "I never heard anyone yell so loud before," he said. Then he smiled at her, as though she had done something special.

"This is Smokey's mother, Martin," Franny said.

Martin's smile grew even wider. "I love Smokey," he declared. "Did you know he saved me from getting run over?"

Lena's rage burst out again as she glared at Martin. "So you're the one—it's all your fault!"

Martin ran to Franny, and she put her arms around him and Sarah, both of whom were shocked at the woman's anger. Mrs. Copper coughed, trying to speak, but Franny cut in.

"Mrs. Manning, please go outside. There's nobody here to yell at but a sick lady and children who've never been yelled at before. I can see now why Smokey got to like it here so well."

"Don't order me, you brat!" Lena darted another angry look at all of them. Then she grabbed her handbag and stomped out the door, her high heels jabbing the veranda steps.

Franny knelt clutching the little ones as though she were a statue, until she heard the sound of the car leaving. Then the tension suddenly broke, and she began to cry.

"Come, honey," she heard Mrs. Copper say weakly. "Come to Aunt Hazel." Franny buried her face in the comfort of that huge shoulder.

Mr. Copper had been out in the fields cutting oats,

and by the time he returned to the house for a cold drink of water, his wife was feeling better.

"Lena was here," was all she said.

He looked at her sharply. "What did she want?"

Mrs. Copper brushed a few crumbs off the kitchen table where the children had been eating cookies. "I guess Smokey wasn't sure he wanted to go back with her. She was upset."

Martin could not help being honest. "She yelled at everybody," he said. "She made Aunt Hazel sick, and we were scared."

It was the first time they had heard Mr. Copper swear, and he quickly muffled the word. "Hazel, is that true?" he asked.

She nodded. "I got too excited, but Franny got my pills for me. I'm all right now."

"Oh, Hazel!" Mr. Copper put his arms around his big wife and hugged her. His face was full of pain. "I've felt sorry for Lena and put up with her because she's my little sister, but this is too much. I'll never forgive her for hurting you."

There were tears in Mrs. Copper's eyes, but somehow she looked very happy.

They heard a car drive in, and for a second Franny was afraid Lena Manning had come back. But it was Gil, dropping off Mama.

Mama's eyes were sparkling and she looked very pretty in her blue dress when she came in the door.

"I've been to see Smokey," she said, smiling. "I think

Gil and I talked him into staying here with you."

Franny stood with her mouth open. At least three different feelings came over her at once. Disappointment that Papa would not be coming back. Relief, knowing that this was really the best decision for everyone. But most of all, surprise at her mother, who she had never thought able to talk anyone into *anything* before.

Aunt Hazel started thanking her, but Mama turned to Franny, a little worried again.

"I'm sorry, Franny. I had to do it. It wouldn't have been fair to let Smokey go."

Franny answered with a hug. She looked into Mama's eyes. "I guess I already knew that," she said. "I knew it for sure when I told Mrs. Manning to go away and leave Smokey alone."

"You told Lena that?" Mr. Copper asked admiringly.

Mama smoothed Franny's hair. "I'm sure she did," she sighed. "Franny has a quick temper, like my mother. James has always tried to get her to control it. . . ."

"Well, I'd say this time it came in handy," said Mr. Copper, chuckling.

Martin and Sarah settled into the red wagon again, and Franny and Mama walked up the road slowly. One thought was still troubling Franny.

"The letter to my grandparents, Mama. Are you still going to mail it?"

"Oh, I guess I forgot about the letter. Yes, I'll mail it tomorrow."

"Oh, Mama!" Franny had been so sure that Mama

had changed her mind. "I can't stand having to go live with them, Mama."

"Live with them? Oh, no, Franny. You and everyone else have convinced me to stay here. My letter is an invitation to your grandparents to visit us. If they meet my wonderful children, they might see that I haven't wasted my life after all. And especially if I take that job Miss Spinney offered."

"Yippee!" Franny was so relieved that she dropped the handle of the wagon and threw her arms around her mother's neck. Tears flowed down their cheeks, but they were laughing at the same time.

"Am I really just like my grandmother?" Franny asked, when she had regained her composure.

Mama's smile faded. "No, Franny, you're not. You've proved this summer that *you're* able to forgive. Smokey is going to be very happy to find that out. It's something I wish my mother could learn."

"Maybe I should meet her," Franny said. "I could teach her what it's like to eat crow."

Martin laughed, as though that were a very funny thing to say.

CHAPTER 17

Scrub Oak and Elderberry

Miss Spinney from the county school superintendent's office was coming, and Mama had insisted on having the house spic-and-span. Franny's
knuckles were still red from pushing a scrub brush. As
if clean floors had anything to do with teaching.

"I sure hope Miss Spinney doesn't have hay fever,"
Franny remarked, eyeing the colorful bouquet of wild-
flowers adorning the table.

Mama had been fussing with the freshly washed curtains, making sure they hung right. Her hands stopped
in midair.

"Oh, no! I never thought of that!" she gasped.

"I was only joking, Mama. These few flowers aren't
going to make anyone sneeze. Everything looks nice.

Do you mind if I go over to Aunt Hazel's now?"

Franny had gone every day since her encounter with Smokey's mother. Every time she thought about Mrs. Copper all pale and clammy that day, she could feel caterpillars crawling up her back.

"I suppose you may as well," her mother replied. "Martin and Sarah are napping and Miss Spinney should be here soon. I guess I have everything ready."

Franny closed the screen door quietly behind her and started down the driveway. She had a strange feeling these days that the world was changing around her, too fast for her to keep up. Or was it she who was changing? Would she have thought to close the screen door quietly last May?

She glanced toward her feet. Mama had made her wear the new school oxfords today—in case Miss Spinney saw her—and one of the new dresses they had bought with the money Papa sent.

The dresses were different, too, this year. When she was alone, looking in the mirror, she couldn't help admiring the extra gathers in front—the curving in at the waist—almost as though she had a "figure." But in front of other people, she sometimes longed for a big sweater to hide inside.

Next week, she would be in the seventh-grade room at school, along with the eighth graders. And in February, she would be thirteen. All her life she had wanted to be grown-up. Now that it was really happening, she wasn't so sure. She reached for one of her long braids and ran her fingers along its silky texture. Maybe she wouldn't beg to have them cut, after all.

Across the road, Mr. Copper's tall corn creaked and rustled in the breeze, and in the distance she could hear the drone of his tractor as he brought in the last loads of sweet-smelling hay. Even without Papa, this was a good place to be.

She left the road and walked slowly up the Coppers' dusty driveway. Halfway up the drive, she saw that someone was sitting on the front porch. The familiar wave of hostility surged up when she saw it was Smokey Manning.

But I don't hate him anymore, she told herself. *This time I have to be nice to him.*

Somehow she made herself climb the porch steps. He was just sitting there, with his leg cast resting on a chair, a pair of crutches leaning nearby. He didn't say anything, just watched her climb the steps.

"Hi," she said.

"Hi." His suntan had faded already, and his hands, resting on the arms of his chair, looked pale and weak.

"I didn't know you were out of the hospital." Franny forced herself to look straight into Smokey's dark eyes.

"Gil and his mother brought me home this morning. The doc says I'm healing good."

"I'm glad," Franny said.

"You don't have to lie." There was a glint in Smokey's eyes, like he was ready for one of their fights.

"I'm not lying. Thank you for—for what you did."

"Hey, you're the one to thank. If you hadn't yelled, nobody would have noticed that truck . . ." Smokey winced at the memory. "How's my little Marty doin'?"

"If he'd known you were home, he wouldn't be taking his nap right now, I can tell you."

That was one thing they agreed on. They both loved Martin. Both of them smiled, and the tension relaxed.

Mrs. Copper opened the screen door from the house.

"Oh, Franny. I knew I heard voices. Sit down and make yourself comfortable while I fix us a pitcher of lemonade. It's nice and cool on the porch."

"Don't go to any trouble, Aunt Hazel." The name slipped out so easily now.

"No trouble. Only takes a jiffy." Mrs. Copper disappeared into the house again.

Franny sat down stiffly on one of the shabby wicker chairs. She hated this silence. It had been a lot easier talking to Smokey when they quarreled all the time.

She looked out toward the neat white mailbox by the side of the road, and at the three handsome blue-spruce trees. Nothing to talk about there. She stole a glance at Smokey. He was looking straight at her, with a funny little smile.

"I was just wondering," he said, "why you're all dressed up today. Looks like a whole new outfit."

Franny tried not to look embarrassed. "Mama wanted me to wear my new school clothes when Miss Spinney from the county school superintendent's office came."

"That's right, school's starting next week, huh? I s'pose you've got lots of boyfriends in school."

There was no way to stop the blush she felt spreading across her cheeks. Who did he think she was—Dorothea Davis?

"I don't have boyfriends," she snapped.

"I'll just bet you don't," teased Smokey. "What about Gil?"

"That's different. He's a friend, not a boyfriend. And Charles Webster, too."

"Ha, ha, ha!" Smokey seemed to be enjoying himself. He didn't even look so pale now. "Maybe the boys around here are kind of backward. Back in Milwaukee where I come from, they'd want to be more than 'just friends' with a cute girl like you."

"Oh!" Franny sprang from her chair and rushed through the door into the house, almost running into Mrs. Copper, who was bringing the lemonade.

"My sakes, Franny, what's the matter?"

Franny clenched her teeth and got control of herself.

"I was trying to be nice to him," she muttered. "But that lasted about five minutes. He makes me so mad!"

"There, there. Come back out with me. Smokey just likes to tease. In fact, it sounds like he's back to his old self. That's what I missed about him when he was feeling so poorly."

Reluctantly, Franny followed Mrs. Copper back to the porch, but she refused to look at Smokey.

"Smokey, you'd better apologize. You've got my little Franny all upset again," Aunt Hazel said as she handed him a big glass of lemonade.

"Aw, I'm sorry, Franny." She could tell from his voice he wasn't. "See, Aunt Hazel, she was being such a perfect lady, she just didn't seem like Franny. I couldn't resist finding out what it would take to get her dander up again."

Franny pretended she was a queen observing a garden slug, but as she tried to stare him down, the friendly laughter in his eyes won her over, making her smile. For the first time, she saw something to like about Smokey Manning.

"Now, that's better," said Mrs. Copper, settling herself into the sagging sofa and taking a long sip of her lemonade. "It seems good to have time to sit down and enjoy you youngsters. Soon you'll both be off to school and—"

She broke off and glanced quickly at Smokey, whose laughter had suddenly been replaced by a frown.

"I guess I spilled the beans, didn't I?" she grimaced.

Smokey shrugged and said nothing.

"Well, what the heck, why don't we ask Franny what she thinks? She's got a good head on her shoulders."

"If it's a secret, I don't want to—" Franny began, but Smokey interrupted.

"I don't mind. Tell her, Aunt Hazel."

"We've been thinking—Carl and me—Smokey has

come to be just like a son to us, and in a few years we'd like to retire and let him take over the farm."

Franny couldn't see why that should make Smokey so gloomy.

"There's a catch," Smokey muttered.

"It's no catch. It's an opportunity," insisted Mrs. Copper. "Carl knows what he's talking about and he says things are going to be changing in this country. They're already coming up with all kinds of newfangled ideas about agriculture. A good farmer is going to have to know which side his bread is buttered on. He's going to need an education."

"They want me to go to college," Smokey said.

"College! That's wonderful," Franny exclaimed.

"Maybe for some people. But I never gave any thought to it at all. I said bye-bye to high school two years ago and was mighty glad to graduate. All that studying. . . ." Smokey shook his head. The dark waves slipped toward his forehead, but he didn't bother to comb them back.

"Your grades weren't too bad," his aunt said, "except for all them unexcused absences. But that was because you were just a kid."

She turned to Franny. "He won't be much help to us on crutches this fall, so we figured it was a good time for him to start."

"Why don't you want to go, Smokey?" Franny asked softly.

"I don't know—I'm happy where I am—lots of reasons. . . ." Smokey hesitated. Then he sighed and looked her straight in the eye.

"The truth is that I don't know if I can do it," he said. "If I flunk out, I'll be letting everybody down."

Franny stared right back at him. "In that case," she said, "I guess you're right. It would be really stupid to try." She took a long drink of lemonade and looked at him again. "Only I'm just glad Gil didn't think like that this summer."

Smokey managed a crooked smile. "You've got an answer for everything, haven't you, Miss Smarty?"

"I wish I did," she answered.

Mrs. Copper was never one to shilly-shally, but right now, Franny could see that she wanted to say something but didn't know how. Franny waited for her to find the right words.

"Franny," she finally said, "I'd appreciate it if you didn't mention this to your mother. We don't want to get her hopes up. . . ."

The seed of optimism that Franny had buried bloomed into a wild hope. Smokey must have seen it on her face.

"Don't you get your hopes up, either, Franny," he said. "I hate to be the one that always messes things up for you. But I can't decide this for Uncle Carl or for Aunt Hazel or for your father. Julia Jarvis is taking me to Madison next Monday to talk to some people at the

Ag School. I got to know what I'm getting into. And then I have to decide for *myself.*"

Franny stood with her eyes lowered and bit the edge of her lip.

"So I guess if you end up hating me again, I'll just have to stand it," he added.

"I'll try not to," Franny said. "Not for that, anyway. But just don't go around saying I have boyfriends."

Fun flooded Smokey's face again.

"Then I can't help it if you're mad—I meant every word I said."

Miss Spinney's car was still parked by the house when Franny returned. She decided not to barge in right then. Mama and Miss Spinney probably had a lot to discuss. Besides, it gave her a good excuse to head for the elderberry thicket.

Ignoring the bold squirrels that scurried in circles, in their agitated acorn games, she found her favorite mat of long grass and plunged into it.

Excitement had been building up inside her ever since the conversation with Mrs. Copper and Smokey. She hardly dared think about it, but what if Smokey did decide to go to college? It would be a dream come true to have Papa back, working for Mr. Copper.

It was going to cost the Coppers a lot of money to send Smokey to college. But Charles had said people like the Coppers had money even in bad times. Maybe they just felt it was time to spend some of it.

On the other hand, Smokey might decide to turn down the offer. And she knew he was right. He had to make that decision for himself. Whatever it was, now that she knew him better, she wasn't going to blame him for it.

"We'll make it, Papa. One way or another," she whispered.

Franny turned and pressed her cheek against the rough trunk of the tree behind her. It occurred to her why she loved this spot so much. Scrub oak and elderberry bushes—they were rough, tough, and resilient—just like the Parsons family.